BOOK of legion

Smoke & Honey

ja huss

BADLANDS MC
BOOK 4

Book of Legion - Badlands MC #4
A Dark Outlaw Biker Serial Romance

SMOKE & honey

New York Times Bestselling Author
JA HUSS

SMOKE AND HONEY

Copyright © 2026 by JA Huss
Cover design by JA Huss
Interior design by JA Huss
ISBN: 978-1-957277-63-9
All rights reserved.

No part of this book may be reproduced in any form or by any electronic or mechanical means, including information storage and retrieval systems, without written permission from the author, except for the use of brief quotations in a book review.

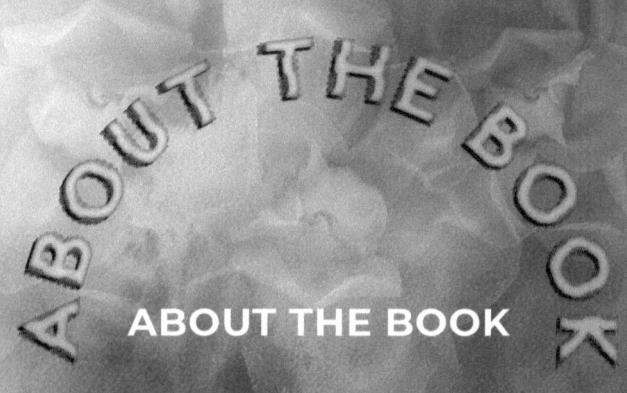

ABOUT THE BOOK

In this war between heaven and hell, someone has to bleed. Legion Kane understands this to his core. He's spent his whole life being trailer trash with no future.

Savannah Ashby was a dream. Perfection wrapped up at designer prairie dresses and equestrian boots. An angel to his demon.

And now, she's his savior.

After being haunted by Eleanor, stuck in a looping memory of days gone by, Legion suddenly finds himself living the high life at the Ashby Ranch. Watching Mercy be spoiled by Cash like he's got some kind of claim on her.

Hardest part is… spoiled looks good on his baby sister.

Ashby money is something Legion will never have.

Ponies and presents.

Princess in training.

Dynasty wealth.

Always on the outside lookin' in.

SMOKE AND HONEY

Where the right side of the tracks meets the wrong side of everything.

Inside the pages you can expect:
- 🏍️⛓️🔥 Outlaw Biker Romance
- 💎🖤🔧 Rich Girl / Poor Boy
- ⛓️🔒🖤 Property Of
- 🖤🫦🗡️ Morally Gray/Anti-Hero MMC
- 🔥👁️⛓️ Obsessed/Possessive MMC
- 🚫🖤🫦 Forbidden Love
- 👩‍❤️‍💋‍👨💍🖤 Only Her
- 🖤🗡️👬 Only Him
- 💚🏡🌿 Childhood Sweethearts
- 🗡️🔪💀 Touch Her and Die
- 🔥🌶️😖 Primal Spice
- 🤐🔒🖤 Secret Relationship

CHAPTER 1
LEGION

My name has always felt like a warning.

Prophetic and foreboding at the same time.

There are demons inside you, Legion.

Not one or two, but Many.

We are many…

I get it. It's not a good start to life, I do agree. But at least I understand it, this demon thing. Because most people think demons are entities. Ghosts. Evil spirits.

But that's not what they are at all.

Demons are regrets. Mistakes. The time you spent off the path because even though you knew—you fucking knew—you were goin' in the wrong direction, you went anyway.

That's what a demon is. It's a mistake that turns into a regret.

And it comes due, the consequences of these mistakes.

Always. They always come due.

I wake flat on my back. My eyes crack open slow,

like they're weighted with lead. The world's a blurry smear, and I blink twice, three times, strugglin' to focus on anything solid.

Light cuts through the wooden slats above me in sharp, dusty beams. Grain dust hangs suspended in the air, swirlin' like smoke in the morning light. Each particle catches fire in the sun—thousands of tiny stars drifting in slow circles. I've seen this ceiling before.

I smile despite the pounding in my head.

This place. This goddamn place.

Outside the silo, there's a faint sound threadin' through the quiet—the distant buzz of a dirt bike's engine winding up and down the hills. The sound hits me in the chest harder than any fist.

That sound meant freedom once.

My first bike was a piece of shit Honda with faded plastics and a bent clutch lever, but she ran. Fifteen years old with nothing but that bike and a pocketful of hard-earned cash I'd scraped together nickel by fucking dime.

Most of the time I worked the feed barn. Stackin' fifty-pound bags until my shoulders burned, sweepin' out corn that stuck to my sweat-soaked skin. Sleepin' in the loft some nights when things got too bad at home.

Builds character, hard work like that does. But more importantly, if you're fifteen and a boy who just wants to be a man, it builds muscles. I was always lean, but after that year in the feed barn, I was a monster.

In the spring and summer, I picked up work at the grain co-op. Sweepin' out grain bins in a dust mask, sweatin' in ninety-degree heat. Shovelin' out pits when they got plugged up because no one else would fuckin' do it. It was a terrible job. But it paid. Spring and summer in Drybone was like a salve over the burn of winter. It soothed ya. Made you forget about the minus-forty windchill comin' around the corner.

Then there was the livestock auction in the fall—sortin' calves in freezing wind, moving cattle with hot shots, walking through frozen shit.

And at the end of all that character building that gave me muscles, was the dirt bike.

It was everything to me that summer.

I can still hear it in the distance. Just for a moment, I'm fifteen again. Counting out six-hundred and seventy-five dollars in hard-earned cash. A fist-full of wrinkled bills I'd hidden in a coffee can under the trailer. That feelin' I got when I kick started the engine the first time was somethin' like clarity.

Somethin' that was mine.

Bought and paid for.

Somethin' no one could take from me.

I blink again, harder this time, trying to clear the fog from my head.

Somethin's not right.

I try to sit up, but my body feels wrong—disconnected, like I'm wearing someone else's skin. Not painful, just... off. Like someone took me apart and put me back together with pieces missing.

I look down at my hands. They're mine. Callused palms, knuckles that have seen more fights than I can count, the faded "MERCY" inked across them. The letters worn and blurred from years of throwin' punches and grippin' handlebars. My boots are still on

—scuffed leather. Jeans too, faded and ripped. Worn to perfection.

But I'm shirtless. Bare chest risin' and fallin' with each breath, the sprawlin' tattoos of angels and demons locked in eternal combat across my skin, catchin' the dim light filtering through the silo's rusted walls.

No blood. No bandages. And no brand.

I run my fingers over the spot where the Badlands B should be burned into my flesh, just above my heart. Nothing. Just smooth skin where that iron pressed against me, where Chains held that glowing metal while the brothers stomped their boots in rhythm. The place that had been raw, angry red, still weeping when Savannah touched it last night.

This has got to be a drunk blackout. Wouldn't be the first time I woke up in this silo with gaps in my memory. But this doesn't have the cotton-mouth, head-splitting quality of a hangover. No taste of stale whiskey, no churning stomach. This is somethin' else.

How the fuck did I get here?

I close my eyes, trying to pull the pieces together from the fog. The last thing—the very last thing I remember—was lying in the bunkhouse in room 3 with Savannah's head against my shoulder. She was breathing slow and even as she drifted off. The hum of nothing in the hallway outside our door, just the distant sounds of the club settling for the night.

We'd just gotten back from dinner at the Duns'. Havoc's ribs and warnings. June givin' Savannah a soothin' tour through biker-wife life.

The far-side of twenty-three looking the near-side in the eye.

It was a nice time.

Then back to the clubhouse. Savannah in the shower with me, water running down her body, steam rising between us.

Then bed. Sleep.

But how did I get from there to here?

From warm sheets and her breath on my neck to a dirty floor and empty air in this abandoned silo?

I sit up fully, ignoring the protest in my ribs. The sound hits me again—a dirt bike engine, revving hard, then skidding to a stop just outside. My hand doesn't reach for a weapon. My pulse doesn't spike. That sound is wired into me different.

It carries no warning. No red flags. No flashing lights lettin' ya know that you're about to create regrets.

That sound is freedom.

Then he walks in—me. Fifteen years old. Lean, but not skinny. Not as tall and broad as I am now, but gettin' there. All those new muscles from hauling feed bags. He's wearin' a t-shirt and those faded jeans that came from the Goodwill in Glendive. No tattoos, not yet. Not many scars, either. Shaggy blond hair falling across blue eyes that haven't seen Whitefall yet.

Wow. I haven't thought about this kid in years. Over a decade, easily.

He's got no idea what's coming.

My younger self has a pack slung over one shoulder, canvas and dirt-stained. I know what's in there without looking—a ratty blanket stolen from the hall closet, two warm beers lifted from Deacon's stash, and an orange soda for Savannah, because she loves oranges. If she had a pack or a purse back then, there was always an orange in there.

He chose those items deliberately, planned every silo meeting like it was the most important moment in his life.

There are no demons in this memory, so me, Legion age 32, smiles.

The kid drops his bag in a practiced move I still use—one fluid motion, controlled fall, lands exactly where he wants it. He studies the silo, looking… landing. His eyes catch on a folded piece of paper stuck on a nail in the wooden ladder.

His whole body shifts, shoulders relaxing, mouth curving up at the corners. That smile—fuck, I'd forgotten I ever smiled like that. Like the world might actually be good for five consecutive minutes.

He crosses the concrete floor and pulls the note free. Unfolds it carefully, like it might dissolve if handled wrong.

The smile gets bigger as he reads. I know what it says without seeing it. Savannah's home from that fancy private school on the west coast, and she's already been here looking for him.

For me.

Every day at noon when she's home, that's our time. Our ritual. I came yesterday, first day of her summer break, but she didn't show. Ranch obligations, probably. Eleanor parading her around for photos, Cash makin' her ride the fence line with him. But she came later, found my note, left one of her own.

I wrote: Missed you. Got a surprise. Gonna be a great summer with you at my back.

I always signed them: Me. Not a name or an initial. Just Me.

Like there was no one else in the world who could be writing to her.

I find myself smiling along with the kid. Remembering the weight of that pen, the careful way I would print each letter, trying to make my handwritin' look better than it was.

And her reply—I can see it in my head now, the looping script she'd perfected years ago.

Dear You...

Couldn't get away. Hovering mother and older brothers demandin' my time like they own it or somethin'.

She always wrote like that. Complete sentences in an accent.

I thought that was the cutest fucking thing ever, how she dropped that g and added a little tick at the end in her written notes. That's how she talked too. To me, anyway. Because that's how I talked to her.

Then she said— You're not the only one with a surprise up your sleeve. I got one for YOU. And maybe YOU will feel good against MY back. This summer's gonna be the best... be there tomorrow for sure.

She always signed her notes: S.

Not Savannah.

Just S.

My past unfolds around me, my memory made real as the sound of hooves hits. Me at fifteen steps outside the silo, watching as Savannah Ashby, age thirteen, comes in at a hard gallop, then pulls up dramatically making the dust fly.

She always did love an entrance.

Savannah slides off her horse as it's still hoppin', lands light on her feet. Her boots hit the dirt with practiced grace. She's wearin' dark jeans that have never seen the inside of a thrift store and her hair is pulled back in one long, thick braid that falls down her back, comin' loose from the wind of her own creation.

She looks wild. That's the best part about Savannah, no matter the age. She's never been one of 'them'. She's always been one of 'us'.

"You're late," younger me says.

But at the same moment, she blurts, "Oh, my god! Family! They act like they own me, or somethin'."

They both laugh, as she explains the new horse. "Eleanor sold my fuckin' pony while I was away at school," she announces suddenly, accent thickening with anger. "Can you believe her? Nine years I had that pony, and she just—" She makes a slashing motion with her hand. "Gone. Didn't even tell me 'til I got home."

"Fucking bullshit," younger me agrees.

But then something shifts in her expression. The anger bleeds out, replaced by a reluctant smile. "But then she brought me to the south paddock, and..." She turns toward her new horse, pride straightening her spine. "I was gettin' too big for Patches anyway. And now I have a real horse! Not some quarter horse built for barrels. A thoroughbred. Seventeen hands. Eleanor hired a private trainer from Billings to teach me jumpin'."

The boy walks over to the new horse, runs a hand

down its neck. He doesn't know shit about horses—not really.

But Savannah made him ride with her. That first summer when she was twelve and I was fourteen, she had the pony. I was already too big for that thing—hell, she was probably too big for that thing. But Savannah said it could hold us both because I was skinny.

That skinny burned me, I remember. Probably why I didn't mind the feed store work.

This thought makes me laugh. The things teenage boys do for girls. But it worked. Because this year, that year, back when I was fifteen, Savannah looked at me different and she hadn't called me skinny in a while.

"This is what you meant in your note?" he asks. "About me against your back?"

"Thought we could ride double," she says, suddenly shy. "If ya want."

If I want, I think in my grown-up mind. That offer is a fantasy come true.

Back in time, my smile widens. "Great minds," he says, gesturing toward the dirt bike parked in the tall grass. "Got my own ride now."

Her eyes widen then. "Holy shit, Legion! When and how?" She knew how poor we were. She knew.

"Saved up," he tells her. "Three jobs this past year. Bought it from a guy over in Glendive. Not new, but it runs good."

They stand there grinnin' at each other, both burstin' with the same idea.

"Makoshika," they say together. The nearby state park filled with secret trails, and a gift shop where I bought her a handmade leather bracelet that summer, and secret canyons with sandy ground that feels good under your toes.

We went all over that fucking place that summer. To this day, there isn't a chance in hell I'd get lost in Makoshika. You could drop me off anywhere and I'd find my way out.

We hiked every trail, we saw every canyon, we even found a little spring. In the dead of fuckin' summer, we found water in the badlands. The gift shop people even called us by name because I bought Savannah an orange soda every mornin' when we arrived.

Thinking back now, it was a good way to spend my fifteenth year. I was poor, my family was fucked and about to get fucked harder, and I knew this was all bad for my future.

But she didn't care. Before Savannah Ashby was my woman, she was my best friend.

I wouldn't trade it for anythin'.

"You on your horse, me on my bike," fifteen-year-old me says, bringing me out of the other memory.

"Or both on the horse," she counters.

"Or both on the bike," he says, voice dropping a little.

The way she looked at me that day—eyes bright, cheeks flushed—it was all there. Already there. The love.

That's one thing I never doubted—Savannah Ashby loves me.

"This is our summer," I tell her.

It comes from my mouth.

Right in the here and now.

And it was our summer.

But that summer was something else too.

It was the beginning of my demons.

Because my first contact with Badlands MC happened that fall, and once I knew what a MC really was, it was the only reasonable future I had.

The memory shifts, the silo dissolving around me. Suddenly I'm crouched in the brush at Makoshika, late September chill creeping through my worn jacket. My breath forms small clouds in the morning air as I clutch the secondhand shotgun.

I wasn't legal to carry that shotgun—the second thing I bought with my own money after the dirt bike. But who needs rules when your stepdad's a drunk and your mom's practically incapacitated with postpartum depression?

I left before dawn that day, determined to get us a turkey for dinner. We were dead broke. Deacon, the piece-of-shit asshole who called himself my stepfather, found my money stash under the trailer two weeks earlier and took it.

All of it.

There was nothing in our fridge but a sack of potatoes about to go bad, some butter, and some milk.

My mama opened the fridge that morning looking for solace after being up a whole night with fussy, colicky, newborn Destiny and said something like... if we only had a turkey, I'd make us a nice dinner.

Now, my mama had not made me a fuckin' dinner in years at this point. It was frozen mac and cheese or frozen burritos. Never nothin' homemade. She had been depressed after Destiny was born because Deacon took less notice of her, not more.

I pictured that dinner in my head and decided I was gonna go bag a turkey and hold her to it.

I did get that turkey, and she did make dinner. It was a turnin' point, actually. She recovered a bit after that. Got through her depression.

That was also the year I learned how Deacon worked. If he was flush with money, he was somewhere that was not our trailer.

He took my money—all that money I saved up—and left. Didn't come back for weeks.

That's how I learned I could pay him to stay away.

To leave us the fuck alone.

Anyway, the most important thing about that day wasn't the turkey or my mama, it was Brick.

I was crouchin' in the fuckin' shrubs, waitin' on turkeys. It was a good spot overlooking a small clearing where I figured they'd come to feed. I settled in to wait, back against a tree trunk, shotgun across my knees. But no turkeys showed. Not a damn one.

Instead, I heard engines. Motorcycles, three of them. Then trucks—two—rolling in from the access road about a quarter mile below my position.

Men in black leather jackets covered in worn patches climbed off the bikes as the others exited from the trucks. They moved through this little clearing like they owned the place, like they'd been here a million times. There were eight of them. They didn't talk loud or bullshit around. Just short sentences to get a job done.

I wasn't hiding. I... wasn't doing anything but sittin',

waiting on my turkey. So I didn't move. Just stayed real still as they worked.

They started unloading crates from the back of one truck. Then duffel bags from the other. The bags sagged heavy in the middle, guns, I figured.

If that's what they were, it was a lot of weapons. Like these men were preparing for a war or somethin'.

They worked quickly, easily. Transferring everything from the trucks to some kind of bunker built into the hillside that I hadn't even noticed before they moved some brush and fallen logs out of the way.

As I watched, it hit me hard. I just saw something very fuckin' secret. Somethin' those men would kill over.

That's when one of them finally noticed me.

He walked straight over, aiming his piece at my head.

I held my breath, but I didn't move. I didn't stand up, I didn't explain, and I didn't run.

I just looked him in the eyes.

It was Brick. He was younger then. Tall, lean, with a full beard just starting to show silver. He looked down at me with cold, assessing eyes. "Mornin'," he said, voice quiet as he pressed his gun against my temple.

The metal was cold, his hand did not shake.

"I don't know what you think you just saw, so I'm gonna tell you what you just saw to make sure we're clear. You saw a gun deal, boy. You saw our hidey hole. You saw something you should not have. So you've got two choices, little friend. One—I'm a liar and that's not what you saw at all. Or two—they find your body out here when the snow melts in the spring."

I said, didn't even hesitate, either, "I got no idea what you're talkin' about, mister. I'm here huntin' turkeys and haven't seen shit all day."

He smiled at me. Then he holstered his weapon, pointed off to my left, and said, "Saw some turkeys over that ridge as we came in."

And then he turned and walked back to the group. Said something that made them all look my way, but nobody moved toward me. Brick went back to work like nothing happened.

The next thing I knew, trucks started, bikes fired up, and they were gone.

I bagged two turkeys that day because of Brick.

He fed me and gave me a reason to live all in the span of three minutes and he never even knew it.

Because something changed in me that day.

For the first time in my life, I had a yearnin'. Not the kind of yearnin' I would have for Savannah, that came later. But a yearnin' for power.

That kind of power. Real power. Not the kind Deacon had—the power to hurt people smaller than him, to steal from his own family. But the kind that came from a sort of brotherhood where a man's word— my word—was worth something.

Brick didn't know me. He had no reason to believe me.

But he did.

And I appreciated it.

I wanted in. Wanted to be one of them. After havin' saved enough money to buy a dirt bike and a shotgun. And after havin' saved enough money to have my stepfather steal it from me and stay away for weeks to spend it, I was wiser than I was smart.

Smart men don't join up with outlaw MC's.

But… wise men do.

I bagged those two turkeys, secured them to my pack, and spent the whole ride back picturing myself with those men.

As one of them.

Badlands.

It was everythin' to me.

When I got home, I cleaned the turkeys and then held Destiny in my arms for the first time as Mama made dinner.

She started getting better after that. Started smiling again. Turning back into her old self.

But I was someone else entirely.

I would never speak of that day to anyone.

Not even Brick when I finally met him for real three years later.

CHAPTER 2
LEGION

I'm back in the silo watching myself—fifteen-year-old me—when she appears.

Eleanor Ashby stands beside me in the silo. Not the withered corpse they buried, but Eleanor at thirty-eight, her prime. The Eleanor who photographed me for years. The Eleanor who owned everything, including parts of me nobody else ever touched.

"Hello, Legion," she says, her voice exactly as I remember it—all honey and broken glass.

I don't answer. Can't. My mouth is sand-dry, and my heart hammers against the smooth skin where my brand should be, but isn't. I touch my chest, feel nothing. No proof I ever belonged to anyone.

Eleanor doesn't seem to notice or care about my silence. Her eyes—Savannah's eyes but colder, sharper—follow my younger self as he and Savannah, still excited every time they meet up, even though it's daily that summer, look into each other's eyes.

"Watch," she says, nodding toward the teenagers. "Moments come and go. You're gonna miss it."

Thirteen-year-old Savannah is wearing a blue dress that makes her eyes look electric and her skin glow golden. My younger self can't stop looking at her.

"I remember this day," I say to no one. Savannah and I stand three feet apart, just lookin' at each other. Neither of us able to speak.

"This moment," Eleanor whispers, almost reverent. "This is when everything changed."

My younger self extends his hand. His fingers are callused from barn work, nails broken and dirty. Savannah looks at his hand for a long moment before placing hers in it.

Their fingers intertwine.

I remember the feeling—her skin impossibly soft against mine, her pulse fluttering against my wrist like she was scared.

I remember thinking her hand was so small, wondering how something so delicate could make me feel like I was drowning and breathing all at once.

"You knew, didn't you?" Eleanor asks. "Even then."

The teenagers stare at each other. Not smiling. Not speaking. Just lookin'. Recognizing something in each other that nobody else ever saw.

"Knew what?" I finally manage to ask, though my voice sounds wrong.

"That she was meant for more than you."

God, she's such a bitch.

But she's also right. I did know. Savannah knew it too. We never talked about it, but we understood it sat between us, unavoidable. As futures typically are.

She was an Ashby. I was a Kane. Her life stretched out before her, golden and certain. Mine was a question mark, a dark road leading nowhere worth going.

But that day, holding her hand for the first time, I made a silent promise. Not that I would love her forever—though I would. Not that I would wait for her—though I did. The promise was deeper and impossible.

That I would become someone worthy of standing beside her, not just holding her hand in secret.

Fifteen-year-old me squeezes Savannah's fingers gently. She squeezes back.

"It wasn't love," I tell Eleanor, though I'm not sure why I'm explaining myself to a ghost, or a hallucination, or whatever the fuck she is. "Not yet."

"No," Eleanor agrees. "It was a pledge."

The word strikes me as exactly right. A pledge. A commitment more binding than a promise, more sacred than a vow.

"You pledged yourself to her knowing you would fail," Eleanor says.

I watch my younger self lead Savannah to the blanket. They sit side by side, shoulders touching, hands still linked. They don't speak much. They don't need to.

"I never failed her," I say, the words burning my throat.

Eleanor laughs, the sound echoing off the silo walls. "You've done nothing but fail her, Legion. And you'll keep failing her until she breaks."

My younger self brushes a strand of hair from

Savannah's face. She leans into his touch, her eyes closing briefly.

We spent that entire summer finding excuses to touch. Holding hands while walking through fields. Shoulders pressed together as she read books to me. Her head on my shoulder as we watched clouds drift overhead.

We never kissed. Never did more than hold hands. But every touch felt like a confession, every silence a conversation.

"You held her hand for a summer," Eleanor says. "Then what?"

The scene before us shifts. Summer becomes fall, becomes winter, becomes spring. The silo remains, but we change. I grow taller, harder. Savannah grows more beautiful, more reserved.

Sixteen-year-old me parks a motorcycle outside the silo. Not my dirt bike—a real motorcycle. The Honda Shadow I saved another year to buy, working those same three jobs, pushing my body past exhaustion, sleepin' four hours a night.

I bought it with hard-earned cash, counted out bills at the seller's kitchen table while he watched, suspicious of a kid with that much money. But it was mine. All mine. The first real bike I ever owned.

Sixteen-year-old me waits in the silo, pacing, runnin' his hand through his hair. When Savannah arrives, I stop breathing. Because I know what happens next.

She steps inside, her hair longer now, her face thinner. No longer a child.

Sixteen-year-old me stops pacin'.

Looks at her.

Takes a step forward.

The memory of our first kiss burns through me like wildfire. I can't watch anymore. I turn away, my eyes finding the rusted walls of the silo instead.

That summer I turned sixteen changed everythin'. Not just because of Savannah, though she was part of it. It was the Shadow.

I bought it for three reasons. One. I had the money. Saved all year for it, even while I was paying Deacon to stay away.

Two. It was street legal. Which was better than a horse and a dirt bike. We'd ride that horse of Savannah's double sometimes. But two teenagers on a horse makes a scene. Two teenagers on a motorcycle with helmets on, do not.

I wanted to take her places. Places that were not a state park. I had big plans for dates. Most of which we never did because we were too busy kissing by that time. Doing bits and pieces of other things too.

But fourteen was too young. I wanted her pretty bad, just… not yet.

It was another year before we slept together. The summer I was sixteen was practice for that.

Third. A boy could not join a MC if he didn't have a fuckin' bike. Even if it was just a shitty Honda, it was better than a dirt bike.

I rode it into Terry, Montana almost every day that summer, got a job at their grain mill instead of Drybone's.

There was no way to bump in to the Badlands crew in Drybone. They just didn't go there. I'd been tracking them for months after that first encounter with Brick.

Watching. Learning. The clubhouse was somewhere near Terry—I'd figured that much out from following their bikes at a distance, seeing which roads they took. I made myself a fixture in town, a local face, even though I still slept at home.

"You were hunting them," Eleanor says beside me, her voice almost admiring. "You wanted to be one of them."

I don't answer. I don't need to. She already knows.

After working at the Terry co-op for two months, I realized my mistake. Outlaw bikers don't frequent grain mills. They weren't gonna magically appear while I was sweeping floors and stacking bags. The men who worked there were decent enough—quiet, hardworking types who minded their business and expected the same from me. But they weren't bikers, that's for sure.

So I quit and got a job at a garage in Terry instead. Parts driver. It didn't pay as well as the co-op, but I didn't care about the money anymore. I cared about positioning. The garage was on the edge of town, the kind of place that didn't ask too many questions about who you were or where you came from.

Most of the mechanics were Northern Cheyenne from the reservation. They spoke their language to each other, switching to English only when they needed to talk to me. They treated me like a ghost—there but not there. I didn't mind. I watched. I listened. I picked up words here and there. Enough to understand when they were talking about bikes or customers.

The first time a Badlands member came into the shop, I almost missed him. No cut, no patches. Just a tall man with a long black braid and coveralls so stained with grease they might have been black originally.

Ratchet.

I didn't know his name back then, obviously, but I recognized his face. He was there that day out at Makoshika. Not the one who held the gun to my head —that was Brick—but one of the others. Loading crates into the bunker.

He paused when he saw me, just for a second. A slight narrowing of the eyes, a tilt of the head.

I kept my face blank, but inside, my heart hammered against my ribs. This was it. The connection I'd been looking for. The way in.

Ratchet said something in Cheyenne to one of the other mechanics, who laughed. Then he walked past me like I didn't exist, heading straight for the manager's office.

I knew I'd been made. Known and categorized. I should have been scared, but instead, I felt a thrill run through me. I was on their radar now.

I turn back to face Eleanor's ghost, her presence as unwelcome now as it was the past. Even back then, she was hunting me. Following me. Watching me. Not just with Savannah, but everywhere.

She showed up outside the parts store in Terry one afternoon. I was loading boxes into the back of the delivery truck when I spotted her across the street. Camera in hand, as always. But she wasn't taking pictures then. She was waiting for me.

When my shift ended, she approached me in the parking lot. Pulled an envelope from her bag and handed it to me without a word.

Inside was a photograph. Me and Savannah in the silo. Our first kiss. Me sixteen, her fourteen. Her hands on my face, my fingers tangled in her hair. The moment captured in perfect, terrible detail.

"Savannah will love you forever," Eleanor said, her voice soft but her eyes hard. "No matter who she marries. Take solace in that."

The meaning was clear. Savannah is not yours. Will never be yours. You can have her heart, but not her life.

I was so angry I couldn't speak. How did she get that picture?

Later, I would go check the silo for cameras, but she'd gotten them out. That was her only chance to get us like that. Inside the silo doin' what we do.

And she knew it.

She burned her bridge to give me that photo.

Why? I never knew.

"You look angry," ghost-Eleanor says now, watching me remember. "You were angry then, too."

"You invaded something private," I say, the words coming out rough. "Something that wasn't yours to see."

Eleanor smiles, that same cold smile I remember. "Nothing is private, Legion. Not in this world. Not with my daughter."

I stare at Eleanor's ghost, my chest rising and falling too fast. Every memory of her, every secret exchange between us, pulses through my mind.

"You had no right," I tell her. "No fucking right to any of it."

Eleanor tilts her head, studying me like I'm something behind glass. Just like she always did. "To what, exactly?"

"To photograph us in the silo. To follow me. To make me—" I stop, the words tangling in my mouth.

"Make you what?" Her smile spreads slow, knowing. "Love me?"

The accusation hangs between us. I want to deny it, but the truth is worse than whatever she thinks. She was there when no one else was. She showed up. My own mother was drowning in her own mind half the time, and when she wasn't, she was working double shifts or dealing with Deacon's bullshit.

"You were a predator," I say finally. "You hunted me."

"And you let me catch you." Her voice stays even. "Over and over again."

I shake my head, but the denial feels hollow. "I was a kid."

"You were never just a kid, Legion. You were always more." She steps closer, and I can almost smell her perfume—something expensive, with notes of roses. "You came to me when I called. You posed when I asked. You took the money I offered."

"I needed that money."

"Did you need the attention, too?" She arches an eyebrow. "The praise? The way I looked at you like you were worth something?"

This question hits. I did need the attention. Craved it, even. In a world where I was invisible at best and a problem at worst, Eleanor saw me.

Like... really saw me. In a way no one else ever did, through the lens of a camera.

"You made me love you," I say, the words burning my throat.

She laughs, the sound echoing in the empty silo. "I didn't make you do anything, Legion. You just knew it was real. So you figured… why not? Why not do more than tolerate the woman who really raised you. Why not love her back."

The worst part is, she's right. I knew what she wanted, what she was doing. And I let her do it. Because she was there. Because she gave a damn when no one else did.

"You know why I did it. You've known for fourteen years, Legion."

Eleanor's ghost stands before me in this strange memory-silo, her smile cold and knowing. She waits for me to speak, like she always did—setting the trap, then watching me step into it.

"You made a deal with me," she says finally. "When you were seventeen."

I didn't want to remember this. Any of it. But the memory rises anyway, thick and choking.

Eleanor found me at work one day. She waited in her Range Rover across from the garage, engine running. I pretended not to see her at first. But she didn't leave. Just sat there, patient as death.

When my shift ended, I walked over. Not because I wanted to. Because I knew she wouldn't go away until I did.

"Get in," she said.

I got in. The car smelled like her—expensive perfume and leather. She drove us to a lookout point outside town. No one around for miles. Just us and the Montana sky.

"I want to tell you about your father," she said.

I stared straight ahead, heart pounding. "I don't have a father."

She laughed. "Everyone has a father, Legion."

"Not me."

"His name was Matthias," she said, ignoring my denial. "Matthias Kane. He came through Drybone on a motorcycle when I was twenty-three."

I didn't look at her. Didn't want to give her the satisfaction. But I listened. How could I not?

This woman had a piece of my history. Something that didn't belong to her, but she had it nonetheless.

And she was gonna give it back to me.

"He stayed six months. Long enough to charm half the town. Long enough to make promises to your mama, marry her, and then leave her pregnant." Eleanor's voice softened. "Long enough for me to fall in love with him."

That got my attention. I turned to her, searching her face for lies. "Love with him?"

"I loved him more than anyone," she said. "Except maybe your mother."

I shake my head. Pushing these things away.

"I have proof." She reached into the back seat and found an envelope, then handed it to me.

I pulled the photo out slowly. Revealing a man on a motorcycle. He was tall, lean, with my exact jawline and blue eyes. His hair was longer than mine at the time, but the same dirty blond. He wore a leather jacket with patches I didn't recognize.

"That's not proof of anything," I said, but my voice shook.

"I'll tell you everything I know about him," Eleanor

said. "Every detail. Every story. But I need something from you in return."

I scoffed.

Of course, she did. That's how Eleanor Ashby worked. Quid pro quo.

But the photo was too tempting to say no. That's why she dangled it in front of me like a carrot. It was bait. "What do you want?"

"Pose for me. Let me photograph you."

I handed the picture back. "No, thanks."

"You don't understand." Her voice hardened. "I'm offering you your history, Legion. The part of yourself you've never known."

I got out of the car then. Walked back to town in the dark. But the damage was done. She planted the seed.

Two days later, I found an envelope on my motorcycle seat outside the trailer. Inside was another photograph of my father. Younger this time. And a note: He loved thunderstorms. Would stand outside in them, face turned up to the rain.

I crumpled the note. Threw it away. But I remembered every word.

The next week, another envelope. Another photo. Another detail: He could play the guitar. Knew every Johnny Cash song by heart.

It went on like that for months. I never agreed to her deal. Never said yes. But whenever I saw her, I... stayed. I didn't run. I let her take her stupid pictures.

And in return, she fed me pieces of a man I never met.

"You were never paid," ghost-Eleanor says now, reading my thoughts. "Not for the photographs."

"No." The word tastes bitter. "Just information. Scraps about a man who left before I was born."

"You wanted to know him."

"I wanted to know where I came from." I look away from her, at the dust motes dancing in the silo light. "If I was like him."

"You are," she says softly. "In all the ways that matter."

I don't ask what she means. I don't want to know.

"I remember the first time I held you," Eleanor says, swayin' the conversation into a new direction. Her voice goes dreamy, lost in memory. "You were nine months old. Your mother was in the drugstore, and she dropped her purse. Everything spilled out—her wallet, keys, lipstick. She was counting change to pay for medicine.

"You were crying," Eleanor continues. "Red-faced with fever. An ear infection, your mother said. I offered to hold you while she gathered her things. You stopped crying the moment I took you in my arms."

I close my eyes, not wanting to hear more. But she keeps going.

"I gave you back, of course. And I paid for the medicine before I left. But on my way out, I thought—he would be so easy to love. A child that wasn't mine, but that didn't matter."

"So you stalked me," I say, anger rising. "Took pictures of me from a distance."

"At first, yes." She doesn't deny it. "I kept my distance until you were older. But I watched you grow up, Legion. I saw you become the man you are."

"You're sick."

"I'm honest," she corrects. "More honest than you're being with yourself right now."

I shake my head, disgust churning in my stomach. "I never told Savannah about any of this. About you and me."

"No," Eleanor agrees. "You kept our relationship separate. Apart from what you had with my daughter."

"It wasn't a relationship, Eleanor."

"Wasn't it?" She raises an eyebrow. "You came when I called. You let me photograph you. You listened to my stories about your father."

"I never agreed to any of it," I insist. "I just... whenever I saw you, I stood still. That was all."

And, technically, what I'm tellin' her is the truth. I stood still while she took her pictures. There was no discussion. Not at that time. She captured me in her camera and then I'd find something. A note stuffed in my jacket pocket or attached to my motorcycle handlebars with a rubber band. It went on like that for a whole year. The stories about him trickled out like that.

"You got what you wanted," Eleanor says. "And I got what I wanted."

I got what I wanted, all right.

An excuse. A way to justify this cravin' I had for the outlaw life.

Eleanor's ghost moves closer to me. "The first time I saw you on that Honda Shadow, I thought he was back from the dead. You looked so much like him, it hurt to breathe, Legion."

I turn away from her, unable to bear the naked emotion in her eyes. This is what I never told Savannah.

How her mother loved a ghost, and saw him every time she looked at me.

Is this what's in store for Savannah if she and I stay with it. If we don't give up. If we make good on that pledge we said only with our eyes that first time we held hands.

Will I turn into my father, causing her to turn into Eleanor?

Or will she become something less?

Truth be told, it's the second one that scares me.

I don't want her to be something less.

I want her to be something more.

CHAPTER 3
LEGION

The silo walls start to blur around me, like someone's takin' an eraser to the edges of everything. The grain dust that's been dancin' in the light freezes mid-air, suspended like stars in a dead sky. Eleanor's ghost flickers at the corners, her form dissolvin' into something less substantial than memory.

"Legion," a voice cuts through. Not Eleanor's. Not the past. "Legion, please. Your fever's too high, baby. You gotta come back to me."

Savannah.

Adult Savannah. Her voice breaks through whatever this is—hallucination, fever dream, death. The panic in her tone feels like cold water splashin' against my consciousness.

"They're sayin' the infection's reached your bloodstream," she continues, words comin' from everywhere and nowhere. "You need to wake up now."

Eleanor's ghost disappears completely. The silo walls start to fade, and something else bleeds through—

the rhythmic beep of machines, the squeak of shoes on linoleum floors, the clinical smell of antiseptic cuttin' through the grain dust.

I don't move. Can't move. My body feels anchored to a different reality than my mind. The brand on my chest—the one that was missin' in the memory place—burns with real fire now. Not the ceremonial kind. The kind that kills.

"Mr. Kane, can you hear me?" Another voice. Clinical. Professional. "If you can hear me, try to open your eyes."

I don't. Not yet. There's somethin' unfinished here. Somethin' I need to see before I can go back. The infection might be killin' me, but this journey through memory feels just as vital. Like if I don't finish it, I'll lose somethin' more important than my life.

I'll lose myself.

The hospital sounds warp and dim as I push them away. The silo begins to rebuild itself around me, grain dust resuming its slow dance in the light. But it's different now. Less solid. The edges of everything have a transparency to them, like I'm seein' through the thinnest veil.

I feel time pressin' down. Whatever grace period my mind's been given is runnin' out. The light in the silo shifts, shadows extending across the concrete floor. Afternoon moving into evening. My time here fadin'.

I stand in the Terry Garage parking lot, sweat soaking through my shirt like I'm under a goddamn waterfall. The midday heat beats down on the asphalt, making the air shimmer and warp.

My stomach growls, reminding me I haven't eaten since yesterday's half-sandwich at the garage where I work full time now for part-time pay.

Just as I'm lifting the last box of parts off the truck, a gleaming white Range Rover pulls into the lot, kickin' up dust that settles on my already filthy jeans. I don't need to see the driver to know who it is.

Eleanor fuckin' Ashby.

"Not now," I mutter, turnin' away like I don't see her. "Go away."

My life's a goddamn mess this summer. Savannah didn't come home at all—off at some fancy horse camp in England with people who probably wipe their asses with hundred-dollar bills. It's like that girl exists in some parallel universe that occasionally crosses with mine, just enough to remind me of what I can't have.

And now her mother shows up, probably wanting to take more pictures of the poor kid from the wrong side of the tracks. Like I'm some fuckin' zoo animal she's studying.

But when Eleanor steps out of her luxury SUV, there's no camera in her hand, just a yellow envelope.

"Legion," she calls, her voice carrying across the parking lot. I wince when the guys in the garage—previously ignoring me like I'm invisible—suddenly look over, taking an interest in whatever's about to unfold in the parking lot with the local poor kid and the Ashby Queen. "I was just passing through and saw you."

Passing through Terry, Montana?

Right. I almost laugh.

She walks toward me with that confidence rich

people have—like the world was built for them to move through it.

"Happy birthday," she says, holding out the envelope.

I freeze with my hand on the truck door. Nobody else remembered. Not my mama, who's been working doubles and sleeps when she's home. Not little Destiny, who's only three and spends most of her time hiding from Deacon's moods. Certainly not that bastard Deacon himself, who's been demanding more and more of my hard-earned cash to stay away from our trailer.

I'm flat out broke these days and it's really starting to piss me off.

The Badlands crew hasn't noticed me either, despite working at the Terry Garage for over a year. I've been trying to get them to let me prospect, but they look through me like I'm made of smoke. A kid on a Honda Shadow with no connections isn't worth their time.

Not even Savannah remembered my birthday.

But who shows up, today, of all days?

Eleanor fuckin' Ashby. Again. Without fail. And I hate her for that—for being the one person who sees me when nobody else even bothers to look.

I sigh and take the envelope, my dirty fingers leaving smudges on the crisp paper. Inside are photographs and five stacks of twenty-dollar bills bound with a paper band that reads, $2000.

Ten thousand dollars. I look at Eleanor. "What the fuck is this?"

"It's money, Legion. And photographs. Don't you want to look at them?"

I let out a breath, removin' the photos from the

envelope. It's a nice stack of five by sevens. Most of them are of me—moments of my childhood I'd forgot about long ago. Me on my shitty BMX bike. Me skippin' stones across the creek. Me standing on a ridge at sunset. The pictures in my hands are anchors to my youth. I grow up before my eyes.

But it's the last photo that stops time.

It's a man with my jawline, my eyes, my build. But older, harder, with a beard and the thousand-yard stare of someone who's seen too much.

My father.

I look up at Eleanor. "Why are you doin' this to me?"

"Doing what?" Eleanor asks quietly.

"Killin' me like this. Why do you wanna kill me like this, Eleanor? Why can't you just leave me alone?"

She frowns. Like my words actually mean something, though I doubt they do. "They're just some of my favorite photos of you. And some money. I meant it as a birthday present, but... but you can consider it payment for all the modeling you've done over the years if it makes you feel better."

I don't react. Don't thank her. Don't smile. My face stays stone as I toss the envelope onto the passenger seat of the truck I drive to pick up parts.

Then I go back to unloading the truck bed like she isn't even here.

"I won't be around for a few weeks," Eleanor says, shifting her weight from one expensive shoe to the other. "I'm... taking a series of photographs in... Wyoming. The light there is extraordinary in late summer."

I don't look at her. Don't acknowledge her words.

Just keep workin', the muscles in my arms and back flexing with each lift and turn.

"Legion," she tries again. Her voice has an edge of desperation that makes my skin crawl. "I'd like to talk about—"

"Got work to finish, Eleanor," I cut her off, still not looking at her. "Thanks for the money and... whatever. Thanks."

She lingers for another minute, then walks back to her Range Rover.

I don't watch her leave, but listen to the engine as it purrs to life, and she pulls away.

The next morning, I'm standing in the Harley dealership in Billings before they even flip the sign to OPEN. The salesman, a paunchy guy with a goatee and a Sturgis Rally t-shirt, eyes the neatly bundled stacks I place on the counter with open suspicion.

"Where'd you get this kind of money, son?" he asks, thumbing through the bills like they're a deck of cards.

"Saved it," I lie.

"Uh-huh," he says, not believing me for a second. "And you're how old?"

"Eighteen," I answer, sliding my ID across the counter. "As of yesterday."

He looks at the license, then at me, then back at the money. "Well, let me count this again, just to be sure."

He counts out every bill, taking his sweet ass time like he's hoping I'll get nervous and confess to robbing a bank.

I don't. Because I didn't.

Eleanor. I thought about her all fuckin' day after she left. Something wasn't right about her, and it's bugging me, but I can't put my finger on what, exactly, it was.

"All right," Sturgis Shirt says. "It's all here."

"Told you it was," I mumble. But he doesn't hear me.

The paperwork to trade in the Honda takes another hour, but when that hour's over, so is my life.

My old life, that is.

Because the Dyna Fat Bob is my ticket in to Badlands.

It's comin'. I can feel it.

The bike is special in that it's a real fuckin' Harley, it's a Fat Bob, and it's black. But other than that, it's pretty average.

But it won't be average forever. And when I throw my leg over it and feel the engine rumble to life beneath me, there it is. The something that's coming roars up inside me and I leave the dealership a different person than when I walked in.

I ride a hundred and eighty-three miles without stoppin', picturing how I will customize the bike. New paint, tank art, replace the dented chrome with matte-black powder coat, ape-hangers, staggered short shots...

It will change over time, and I'll change with it.

The wind tears at my clothes, the sun beats down on my arms, and for the first time in months, I feel alive.

When I finally stop, it's on a ridge overlooking the Badlands compound. From up here, I can see men moving around the property—loading bikes, smokin', passing bottles.

One of them looks up, seems to notice me silhouetted against the sky. But he doesn't point. Doesn't raise an alarm. Just goes back to what he was doin' like I'm not even there.

I'm still invisible to them.

Still nothin'.

But not for long.

These outlaws are my future.

Two years later, the truck stop pavement burns through the soles of my boots, hot enough to fry an egg. Savannah leans over the hood of her Range Rover, spreading out a paper map like we're living in some time before cell phones existed.

Her prairie dress—shorter than anything she'd wear back home where her brothers might see—flutters around her thighs every time a semi roars past.

She bites her bottom lip, concentrating on the blue lines that will take her away from here. Away from me.

I shift my weight, adjusting myself as I watch her. Those legs. That ass. The way her hair falls forward when she bends over the map. I picture walking up behind her, sliding my hands under that dress, bending her over the hood right here in broad daylight. Holding her down with one hand between her shoulder blades while I work her panties down with the other. I'd make her grip the edges of the hood while I spread her legs with my knee. Take my time getting my belt undone, making her wait for it, making her beg for it. I'd fuck her hard enough to leave marks on those perfect hips, her ass slapping against me while truckers honk and her fancy car rocks on its suspension. I'd make her come screaming my name with her cheek pressed against that map, smearing the ink with her sweat, so every time she looked at it, she'd remember whose she really was.

But I don't move. Just stand there with my thumbs hooked in my belt loops, watching her trace highways with her finger.

Two years of barely seeing each other, and now she's leaving for good. The girl standing in front of me isn't the same one who used to ride double on my dirt bike. Her hair's got those expensive-looking highlights now. Her nails are perfect—no more dirt under them from the barn. Even her clothes scream money. Designer shit I don't really understand.

"So I'll go through Denver," she says, tapping the map. "A girl from prep-school lives there and she's gonna ride with me. We'll head east to Virginia. Emory and Henry is here." She points to a spot I don't bother looking at.

It's over. Whatever this thing between us was—if it ever really was anything at all.

"I'll be riding for all their teams," she continues, excitement making her voice higher than normal. "IHSA, IDA, ANRC—"

I don't know what any of those letters mean. Horse shit, that's all I know. Rich-girl shit. The kind of life where you worry about ribbons and trophies instead of whether your little sister ate today.

"Cassia will be delivered to the college stable next

week," she adds, glancing at me like she's waiting for me to care about her fucking horse. "They have the most beautiful facility—indoor and outdoor arenas, trails through the forests..."

I try to picture her there. In that world. With those people. I can't make the image form in my head. These past two years, we'd hook up whenever she came home from that fancy boarding school. Hard, desperate sex in the silo. On my bike. Once in an old barn while a storm raged outside.

But it was just fucking. Never more than that. Never her inviting me to her house. Never me bringing her around my friends. Just our bodies doing what bodies do when they're starving for each other.

Basal instincts. Nothing more.

Our lives split down the middle a long time ago. She went one way, I went another. What's strange is that Eleanor didn't split with her daughter. While Savannah was getting ready to leave me behind, Eleanor was digging her way deeper into my life.

She set up a photography studio in Glendive. From the outside, it looks like a tourist trap—somewhere to buy overpriced prints of Makoshika State Park to hang in vacation cabins. But inside, in the back room with the blackout curtains, she takes pictures of me. The kind I never thought I'd let anyone take.

In most of them, at least lately, I'm completely naked. She positions me careful, though. Makes sure nothing too explicit shows. But her eyes are on me the whole time. Moving over every inch of my skin. Watching me. Seeing parts of me nobody else does these days.

She pays me for it, but only when I ask. I still can't figure out what that means. Does she think I'm not worth paying unless I remind her? Or does she not want to pay me because to her, what we do isn't business? The way she looks at me sometimes makes me think it's something else to her. Something personal. My body is her passion project. But I can't tell for sure.

Back at the truck stop, Savannah folds her map against the creases, shoving it into her purse.

"So, we'll stay in touch, right?" she asks, her voice suddenly uncertain.

I nod, knowing damn well I won't. My phone vibrates in my pocket. Diesel's third message today.

Savannah moves past me toward her driver's door. Our fingers brush for half a second. Not a kiss goodbye. Not even a hug. Just awkwardness hanging between us like we've never fucked under the moonlight in a field of tall grass.

Like we're strangers now.

She climbs into her Range Rover, and I can hear the air conditioning kick on full blast as the engine purrs to life.

I stand there, watching her pull away, the dust kicking up behind her tires. I keep watching until the dust settles back to the ground. Until there's no sign she was ever here.

Then I mount my motorcycle, kick the stand up, and fire the engine. The vibration between my legs drowns out everything else in my head. My phone buzzes again in my pocket.

It's Diesel, I know this. But I didn't wanna look at

the text until Savannah was gone. Until it was really over.

Until there was no goin' back.

Tonight, the gates open for me.

Tonight, Badlands lets me prospect.

As Savannah drives toward her future, she releases me to mine.

The compound gates swing open as I approach as security cameras track my movement, little red lights blinking like hungry eyes. Three years ago, I'd have felt something about that. Pride, maybe. Or fear. Now I just feel the weight of being watched.

Twelve Harleys line the parking lot in perfect formation—chrome polished, leather oiled, each one angled precisely the same way.

I park my bike off to the side. Not part of the formation. Not yet.

Inside the clubhouse, the smoke hangs thick enough to walk on. Cigarettes, weed, something else burning that I can't name. A pool game stops mid-shot, cue ball frozen in its trajectory. Laughter cuts off like someone pressed mute. Every eye finds me.

Diesel emerges from the back hallway, his bulk taking up more space than seems possible. He's got grease under his fingernails and a fresh cut above his eye. No explanation offered for either. He tosses a rag at my chest. I catch it without thinking.

"About fucking time," he says, but there's no welcome in it.

Roach points toward a dark stain on the concrete floor with his chin. Blood. Not fresh, but not old enough to have set completely. Beside it a bucket of water—smells like bleach.

I don't ask questions. Questions are for people who have the right to answers.

My stomach growls as I head towards the stain and kneel down, the floorboards hard against my knees.

And then I start scrubbing.

My back muscles strain immediately. The blood has dried into the porous surface, requiring force to lift it out. Nobody speaks. Nobody offers help or explanation. I can feel Brick watching me from his chair in the corner, the weight of his attention heavy.

Minutes stretch. My knees begin to ache against the hard floor. The bleach burns my nostrils and the skin on my knuckles. Still, I scrub. Harder. More deliberately. Making each movement count.

Around me, conversations resume. Pool balls crack against each other. Someone laughs at a joke I didn't hear. I've become invisible. A ghost that only exists to perform this task.

When it's clean, I stand, legs stiff from kneeling so long. No one acknowledges the completed task. No one says "good job" or "that'll do." I exist in a vacuum of recognition.

I move to the bar, my boots leaving wet marks where bleach water dripped from the rag. The whiskey bottle sits unguarded. I pour myself two fingers into a dirty glass, aware that every movement is still being evaluated.

No one objects. No one welcomes. The amber liquid catches the dim light as I raise it to my lips.

The whiskey burns all the way down to my empty

stomach. The alcohol spreads through my blood, dulling the edges of hunger and fatigue.

Across the room, Brick rises from his chair. Every eye follows him, except mine. I stare straight ahead, feeling his approach, rather than watching it.

"Kane," he says, his voice gravel and smoke.

I turn, meeting his gaze directly. "Sir."

His face gives away nothing. "You eat today?"

The question catches me off guard, but I don't let it show. "No, sir."

He nods once, like I've confirmed something important. "Diesel, get this boy some food. Can't have him passing out before we've even started."

Diesel grunts acknowledgment, disappearing into the back.

Brick doesn't move away. He stays close enough that I can smell the tobacco on his breath. "You know why you're here, son?"

"To earn my place."

"And what makes you think you deserve one?"

I don't hesitate. "I don't deserve shit. Nobody does. You earn what you get or you take it. I'm here to earn."

Something flickers across his face—not approval, exactly, but acknowledgment. "Your daddy thought the same thing."

The world stops when these words come out of Brick's mouth. I keep my expression neutral, but my pulse kicks up. "You knew him?"

Brick's mouth twists into something that might be a smile on another man. "Oh, I knew him all right."

The room goes silent again, every ear straining to catch this exchange.

I don't know what to say to that.

Brick studies my reaction. "You got any questions for me, Demon?"

Demon.

"No, sir. I don't have no questions. I don't even know who that asshole was. You," I say, nodding to him. "I've known you since I was fifteen." This is the first time I've ever mentioned that day to Brick. Not even sure he remembers.

But when he smiles, I know he does. "Well. You never did say anything about that secret you stole from me. That's why you're here, Demon. That's the only reason you're here. Unlike your father, you know how to keep your fuckin' mouth shut."

I don't know what to say to this, so I figure nothin' is best. But I file it all away. It's a part of me now, this history with Brick and Brick's history with my father.

Diesel returns with a plate—beans, cornbread, some kind of meat I don't look too closely at. He sets it on the bar beside me without ceremony.

"Eat," Brick commands. "Then we talk business."

He turns away, conversation over. The others return to their activities, the momentary tension broken. I pick up the fork, suddenly aware of how hungry I actually am.

As I finish eating, I feel eyes on me again. Roach this time, watching from across the room. He nods toward a hallway I haven't been down before.

Time for the next test.

I push the empty plate away and stand, feeling the whiskey and food settling in my stomach.

Whatever comes next, I'm ready.

This is where I belong now.

The hallway stretches dark ahead of me, but I don't hesitate.

I walk forward, leaving the light behind.

The silo dissolves around me like smoke caught in a sudden draft. The dirt floor turns to sterile tile. The sunlight streaming through rusted metal, becomes harsh fluorescent glare.

Beep. Beep. Beep.

I'm floating above myself. Some fucked-up out-of-body bullshit that should scare me, but doesn't. The body in the bed doesn't look like me. Too pale. Too still. Tubes running in and out like he's more machine than man. The brand on his chest—my chest—is an angry red crater, the skin around it swollen and streaked with infection lines that spider outward like lightning.

Savannah sits beside the bed, her fingers wrapped around my limp hand. Her voice reaches me like it's coming through water.

"You promised me, Legion. You said we'd get it right on the backside of twenty-three. Remember? You have to remember."

Her voice breaks on the last word. Her hair is pulled back in a messy ponytail, dark circles under her eyes. She's wearing the same clothes I last saw her in—my t-shirt, those jeans that barely stay up on her hips. How long has she been here?

"The near side too," she whispers. "We're still on the near side, Legion. You can't leave yet."

The door opens. Three people in scrubs enter,

moving with practiced efficiency. One checks the monitors. Another adjusts something in one of my IV bags. The third speaks to Savannah, whose face transforms with relief.

"They're taking you to surgery soon," she tells my unconscious body. "They're going to fix this."

I want to tell her I'm right here. That I can hear her. But my mouth won't move.

A doctor enters, flipping through a chart. "The infection's aggressive," she says. "Resistant to the antibiotics. We're seeing serious signs of sepsis."

"What does that mean?" Savannah asks, her voice small.

"It means we need to remove the infected tissue immediately. Clean out the wound site. Start a broader spectrum antibiotic."

"The brand," Savannah says. "You're cutting out his brand."

"We can't cut the entire brand out—it's too extensive..." I stop listening as the doctor keeps talking. Explaining to Savannah what they're about to do to me.

I notice Mercy then, tucked into the corner chair, her knees pulled up to her chest. Her eyes are red-rimmed, tears streaming silently down her face. She's watching me like she's memorizing my face, like she's already saying goodbye.

Fuck. How long have I been here? How did we get from the compound to—wherever this is?

The room feels crowded now. Too many people hovering over my body, preparing it for surgery. Preparing me. A nurse checks the monitors again, frowning at whatever she sees.

"BP's dropping," she says.

"Let's move," the doctor responds.

Through the open door, I see a figure standing in the hallway. Brick. His face is granite, eyes cold. He watches for a moment, then turns and walks away without speaking to anyone.

In his place, Diesel appears, taking up position outside the door like a sentinel. His massive frame nearly fills the doorway, arms crossed over his chest. Anyone wanting to enter would have to go through him first.

This place—this sterile, beeping, antiseptic-soaked room—is Badlands territory now. Diesel's stance makes that clear to everyone passing by.

Savannah leans over my body as the nurses prepare to move me. Her tears fall onto my face, but the body below doesn't react.

"Please," she whispers. "Please come back to me."

Something breaks inside me at the sound of her voice. The desperation. The fear. I've put that there. Me and my fucking brand. Me and my loyalty to the outlaw family I need and love.

Me and my demons.

I focus everything I have on moving. Just a finger. Just one fucking finger to tell her I'm here. I'm listening. I'm coming back.

And somehow, across whatever divide separates my floating consciousness from that broken body, I feel my fingers twitch against hers.

Savannah gasps. "He moved! His hand moved!"

The nurse closest to her looks skeptical but checks the monitors. "Heart rate's increasing."

I push harder, focusing on turning my head toward Savannah's voice. The effort feels like trying to move a mountain with my bare hands, but slowly, my head shifts on the pillow.

"Doctor!" the nurse calls. "We've got increased brain activity."

Savannah's crying harder now, but different tears. Hope tears. "Legion? Can you hear me?"

I try to open my eyes, but that's still beyond me. Everything hurts now. The floating sensation is gone, replaced by fire in my veins and a crushing pressure in my chest. But I keep fighting. Keep pushing back toward her.

I made a promise. On the backside of twenty-three. On the near side too.

I promised Mercy I'd never leave again.

I promised Savannah, I'd get it right this time.

I even promised myself, seventeen years ago in that silo, that I'd become worthy of her. That was before the demons. Before Badlands. Before prison, and silence, and all the blood on my hands.

I'm not worthy. Never have been. But I'm still here. Still fighting. And that has to count for something.

They're moving me now, transferring my body to a gurney. The ceiling tiles slide past overhead as they wheel me out of the room. Diesel's frowning face appears above me, his eyes unreadable as I pass.

I slip back into darkness, but this time, it's different.

This time, I'm not running from it.

This time I'm comin' back.

CHAPTER 4
LEGION

I wake to white. Just white. My eyes burn from the brightness, and for a moment I think I'm back in The Pit where every once in a while, just for kicks, they'd keep the lights on twenty-four seven.

But this ceiling has tiles. Neat little squares with pinprick holes.

Hospital ceiling.

The room comes into focus slowly—monitors with green lines pulsing, an IV stand with clear bags hanging, chairs sitting empty against the wall. Sunlight cuts through half-closed blinds, hitting the floor at an angle that tells me it's late afternoon. Wrong time of day from what I remember. Wrong quality of light altogether.

My body feels hollowed out, like someone scooped everything important from inside me and left just enough to keep breathing. Thick bandages wrap my chest where the brand sits. I can feel the heaviness of surgical dressing, the pull of tape against my skin.

My hand reaches for my phone without thinking, muscle memory from another life. Not there. Nothing's there. Just thin hospital sheets and the plastic rail of a bed that isn't mine.

The panic hits like a sledgehammer as the heart monitor betrays me, beeping faster, louder.

I try to sit up, and pain shoots through my chest like I've been stabbed.

Fuck this.

I yank the IV from my arm, blood spattering across white sheets as I swing my legs over the edge of the bed. The room tilts dangerously, the floor seeming to rise up to meet me before falling away again.

Alarms start blaring. High-pitched, insistent.

Two nurses rush in, their faces showing professional concern but not surprise. One presses me back against the pillows while the other checks the monitors, silencing the alarm.

"Mr. Kane, you need to stay in bed," the first nurse says, her voice steady. "You've had major surgery to remove infected tissue. Your body needs time to recover."

"Where's Savannah?" I demand, my voice rougher than I expected, throat raw from what must have been a breathing tube. "Where's my sister?"

The nurses exchange a glance I don't like. The kind of look people give when they're deciding how much truth you can handle.

"I'll get the doctor to come speak with you," the second nurse says, already backing toward the door. "He can explain everything about your condition."

"I don't give a shit about my condition," I say, trying

again to sit up despite the first nurse's restraining hand. "Where's my family?"

"Please try to remain calm, Mr. Kane. The doctor will be here shortly to answer your questions."

They both exit quickly, the door clicking shut behind them. I'm alone again with the beeping machines and questions burning holes in my skull.

A little while later the door opens again, but it's not the doctor who walks in.

It's Brick.

He's wearing civilian clothes—jeans, a plain black t-shirt, a baseball cap pulled low over his eyes. No cut or patches. Nothing identifying him as Badlands.

He looks smaller somehow, outside the clubhouse.

Less mythic.

He pulls a chair close to the bed, sits, holds a cup of coffee in his hand as I struggle with reality.

"Where's Savannah? Where's Mercy?"

Brick's face remains impassive, weathered like the side of a cliff that's seen too many storms. He takes a sip of coffee before answering. "That brand got infected. Fever spiked to 104. You started convulsing in your room. Dusty drove you to Glendive Medical Center, but you got worse. Savannah called in Ashby resources—private medical transport to Mayo Clinic. That's where you are now. Minnesota."

"Minnesota?" What the fuck.

"You've been out six days," Brick continues. "Three surgeries to clean the infection. Sepsis hit your bloodstream. They told us you were dying. Actually," he amends. "You did die. Once. For about twenty seconds. But they brought you back. Cash Ashby's involved now," Brick says. Irritation, not sympathy leaking through in his voice. "Called social services on us. You were convulsing pretty much at the same moment they showed up at the Badlands' gate. It was a fucking shit show. Mercy screaming, Savannah screaming. Sheriff fucking yelling at us with a bullhorn. Cash Ashby smirking like the asshole he is as we were carrying you down to Dusty's car. He's the one who reported Mercy living at the clubhouse. Temporary custody hearing happened five days ago."

I try to push myself up again, ignoring the tearing sensation in my chest. "What?"

"Judge granted Cash temporary guardianship of Mercy," Brick says. "Savannah tried to intervene, offered herself as guardian. Court rejected it. She still shares residence with Cash at the Ashby place so there was really no point."

Brick sighs hard and narrows his eyes at me. The only sign of emotion he's shown. "I told you before. I fucking told you, Legion. No goddamn kids at the clubhouse. Now we got social workers, and family court fucking judges, and Cash fucking Ashby eyes all over us."

The rage builds inside me, hot and desperate. I throw back the covers and attempt to stand, but my legs buckle immediately. Weakness overwhelms anger, and I fall back onto the bed, breathing hard.

"I need a phone," I say through gritted teeth. "I need clothes. I need to get the fuck outta here!"

Brick stands, then picks up the hospital phone from

the bedside table and tosses it into my lap. "I'm heading back to Montana," he says. "Two days of waiting to see if you live or die is enough. I've got major shit to deal with, thanks to you."

"Where's Savannah now?" I ask. Desperate for answers before he leaves.

Brick heads toward the door, not looking back at me. "She went back to the ranch with Mercy last night after they said you were gonna pull through," he says. "There's a court date comin' up for Mercy and this one is for keeps."

"Why are you pissed at me? I didn't plan on fuckin' dying over a damn brand."

Brick turns to face me. His expression one of pure rage. "What did you just say?"

I realize my mistake too late. Because... that's literally what the brand means.

I will die for it.

For them.

For Badlands.

I sigh. "You know what I meant."

"All of this is your fault. You didn't take care of the goddamn wound. You didn't take care of Mercy. You didn't take care of shit, Legion. And everyone is about done with your drama. Maybe you're more trouble than your silence was worth?"

Then, without even lookin' back, he walks out.

The door remains open after Brick leaves, hanging there like an accusation. Diesel fills the frame moments later, his massive shoulders nearly touching both sides, face set in that solemn expression I've seen a hundred times before—usually right before someone gets their teeth kicked in.

But there's no violence in his movements as he enters the room, just careful, measured steps that barely make a sound on the linoleum floor.

He places my leather wallet on the bedside table without ceremony, then stands at the foot of my bed, arms crossed over his chest.

"We drove eight hundred miles to check on you," he says, not waiting for me to speak first. "We're heading back today, so I guess that probably sends some signals you might be overthinkin'. But let me say it again, we drove eight-hundred fucking miles to check on you."

No small talk. No how you feeling bullshit.

Just… you owe us. Which is fine. I guess. But a little fucking sympathy would be appreciated.

"Sheriff's been sniffing around the clubhouse since you went down," Diesel continues. "Asking questions about your condition. How you got that brand. Who performed the ritual. They're looking for something, Demon. They don't like you."

"No shit," I sneer. "They don't like any of us."

"No." Diesel shakes his head. "There's something brewing with the Ashby people. I mean…" He sighs. "It's not a surprise, right? I understand you've known each other for decades. I get that the two of you were high school whatevers—"

"That's a joke. She went to prep-school in the Pacific Northwest, Diesel. I quit Drybone High School in the eleventh grade."

"You know what I'm gettin' at," Diesel says. "The

two of you have history. Which only makes this worse, Legion."

"What the hell are you talking about?"

"Her. Savannah Ashby. She's not yours. She's never been yours. She's never gonna be yours because Cash Ashby is gonna make sure of it. And if you fuck with him for too long by fucking with his sister, he's gonna cause trouble. And then…" Diesel shakes his head. "Then… I'll have to take care of it."

"I'm not quite sure what you're sayin' here, Diesel. You're gonna take care of me? Or you're gonna take care of him?"

His response is to place a burner phone on the bedside table next to my wallet. "It's charged, you've got two-hundred minutes and no data. No numbers, either. Brick said—"

But he stops.

Brick said. Brick said, what? Let's brand Legion, give him a false sense of family and security, then cut him out when his life spirals? Fuck Brick."

"Right." Diesel moves toward the door and all I can do is watch him leave. He pauses at the threshold, lookin' back at me. Then he points. "Your head's not in the game. You're my best friend, that's never gonna change. But your head's not in the game. It's always been us or them for you, Demon. Always." He narrows his eyes at me. "And you always chose them."

"Funny," I scoff. "That's not how I see it. I never did time for them."

He scoffs back at me, louder. "I never said nothin' before. Mostly because I didn't care. I believed in you. I trusted you. And fuck it, it just wasn't my secret to share. But I need you to know Legion, that I know why it took you so long to patch in."

"What the fuck are you talking about?"

But he just glares back at me. "I know why, Legion. Why you used to disappear when you were a prospect. I know where you went. And I know who you were with. Because I followed you once."

"What—" But I choke the words off when I realize what he's saying.

I followed you once. His chin tips up. Daring me to contradict him.

He doesn't say anything else.

Doesn't have to.

He made his point.

I followed you once.

The door closing softly behind him feels more final than any slam.

I know three phone numbers by heart.

My landline to the new trailer because it's the same number as the old one.

The clubhouse. Been calling it for over a decade now from sketchy places doing even sketchier things. Burned into my brain from nights when I needed backup, mornings when I needed alibis, afternoons when I just needed someone who understood what the world looks like when you live outside its rules.

And the Ashby residence. Not because I ever called Savannah over there, but because I used to want to, so bad as a teenager, I'd dial the number and hang up before the first ring. Used to practice what I'd say if Eleanor or Cash answered. Used to wonder if Savannah would be allowed to talk to me if I actually let it ring.

Never found out.

These are my choices.

I stare at the ceiling of the hospital room, counting tiles while my chest throbs beneath the bandages. The pain medication makes everything feel underwater, but not deep enough to drown the choice in front of me.

My fingers move before my mind settles, punching in the numbers. Each button press feels like breaking something I can't put back together.

Someone with a Spanish accent picks up the Ashby landline on the fifth ring. Like that phone hasn't rung in so many years, they don't even have it hooked up to an answering service.

"Ashby residence," she says, formal but tired, like she's been working there long enough to know better than to sound excited about anything.

"I need to speak to Savannah," I say, my voice rougher than I expected. This is when I realize my throat is killing me.

There's a pause, a muffled conversation I can't make out. Then rustling, like the phone's being passed around.

"Who is this?" The voice is male, cautious. A butler? A gardener? A ranch hand? Who the fuck knows.

"Put Savannah on the phone," I repeat. Practically growling. "It's Legion."

More muffled voices, sharper this time. I hear her name repeated, then footsteps, the sound of a door closing.

"Hello?" Her voice hits me like a fist to the chest, making the monitors beside my bed beep faster.

"It's me," I say, because what else is there?

"Legion? Oh my God, Legion!" Savannah's voice breaks through the line, breathless, happy, loves me. "Thank God. I've been praying so hard. The doctors wouldn't tell me anything after I left. Just that you were stable. That's the only reason we left. How are you? Are you okay? When did you wake up?"

I can't get a single word in, but I start to smile despite myself. Despite everything. Her voice sounds like the only real thing in this sterile room.

"I'm alive," I manage to say when she pauses for breath.

"Barely," she says, and I can hear the worry beneath her relief. "But don't worry, they're gonna release you into my team's care in three days. Just hold tight."

My smile fades. "What?"

"My team. The medical team I hired. They've been coordinating with your doctors."

I don't know what that means. My brain feels like it's working through mud, trying to make sense of her words.

"Savannah, what are you talking about? What team?"

"The only way they'll discharge you is if you have somewhere to go where you can receive IV antibiotics around the clock, or you'll relapse and the infection will get worse," she explains, her voice taking on that tone she gets when she's already decided something. "You will die without treatment, Legion. The doctors were very clear about that. You are not better. Only stable."

The monitors beside my bed beep faster again as my heart rate climbs. "OK. Now tell me what you haven't said yet."

"Well..." Her voice brightens, like she's delivering good news. "You're moving into the Ashby Mansion, of course. It's the only place equipped. And anyway, I'm here. Mercy's here. So you should be here too."

CHAPTER 5
SAVANNAH

I've always loved the crow's nest. A circle of windows wrapping three hundred and sixty degrees around a space too small to impress anyone—just big enough to breathe in.

"Is that it?" Mercy presses her nose against the glass, leaving a perfect smudge that would've sent my mother into conniptions. "Is that the helicopter?"

I squint at the distant speck hovering above the eastern pasture. "Not yet, sweetie. That's just one of the crop dusters for the Whalburg place."

Mercy sighs dramatically, her shoulders slumping. "How much longer?"

"Soon." I rest my hand on her shoulder, feeling the bone beneath her t-shirt. She's still too thin, though Cash has been stuffing her with organic everything since the judge handed her over. "Why don't you check on Puddles? Make sure he hasn't destroyed another pair of Cash's boots."

"He only did that once," Mercy says defensively, but

she's already halfway to the spiral staircase, eager to reunite with the golden retriever puppy that materialized within hours of the custody hearing. As if a dog could replace a brother.

Alone again, I press my forehead against the cool glass, taking in the view that used to feel like a kingdom and now feels like a prison yard.

The Ashby Ranch sprawls in every direction—forty-seven thousand acres of Montana that my mother made sure the entire world knew was ours. To the north, the cattle pastures stretch toward the horizon, dotted with Black Angus that look like toys from up here. The eastern fields roll golden with wheat and barley, while the western edge disappears into pine forests that climb toward the mountains. South of the mansion, the outbuildings cluster like a small town. And beyond them, the private airstrip that we don't use much, but maintain just in case.

Ten days ago, I was sitting at the Duns' dinner table, watching Legion laugh with Havoc's kids, feeling like maybe—just maybe—I'd found somewhere I actually belonged.

Then everything went to hell.

The panic when I woke to Legion burning with fever beside me, his brand an angry red against his skin, was the kind where time slows down and you simply can't breathe.

The chaos at the compound gate when the sheriff showed up with that fucking warrant. Cash sitting in his truck, watching it all unfold with that smug half-smile he gets when he's won something.

"Child welfare concerns," the papers said. As if Cash

has ever given a single fuck about any child's welfare, especially not a Kane.

The emergency hearing was a joke. My lawyer—the best money can buy, of course—made all the right arguments. The new trailer on Kane land was as good as any home in this county. Brand new and still immaculately clean, the inspection of it the day before the hearing went well. The social worker seemed to think it was the best place for Mercy. I had resources. I had a genuine connection with Mercy. I was perfectly capable of being her temporary guardian in the Kane home while Legion recovered.

Then Cash's lawyer stood up.

"Ms. Ashby has shown severe lack of judgment," he said, like he was discussing a wayward teenager instead of a thirty-year-old woman. "Allowing herself to be lured into an outlaw biker lifestyle, exposing a minor child to criminal elements..."

Lured. That fucking word still burns. Like I'm some helpless princess who couldn't possibly choose a life that didn't involve designer dresses and charity galas. Like I didn't walk into that clubhouse with my eyes wide open, knowing exactly what I was doing.

But I couldn't say that in court, could I? Couldn't stand up and say, "Actually, Your Honor, I chose Legion. I chose his world. I chose to let a man named Chains write 'PROPERTY OF DEMON' across my tits with a Sharpie, I chose to suck his dick in front of fifty people to show my allegiance to him, and I fucking loved every minute of it."

That... though true, is not what a judge wants to hear. Not if I wanted any chance of helping Mercy.

So I sat there, hands folded in my lap, playing the part of the Ashby heiress who'd had a momentary lapse in judgment but was now back where she belonged.

It didn't matter. Cash had already won. The judge took one look at the "brand-new trailer with no established connection" versus the "stable family environment of the Ashby Ranch" and made his decision.

What Cash hadn't counted on was Legion's infection going septic.

Of course the brand looked like shit, and of course, I noticed this when I looked at him. But he seemed fine. Everything seemed fine until his body started shutting down and heating up.

Ten days ago, I barely knew a condition called sepsis existed.

Today, I feel like an expert.

But I didn't see the signs. And Legion, being Legion, isn't the kind of man who complains about pain.

He wanted that brand. To him, it was an honor. It should have made him untouchable. It was a signal to anyone—whether they knew it or not—that Demon Kane was protected.

Instead, it tried to kill him. By the time Dusty and I got him to the emergency room in Terry, his fever was 104, and he was barely conscious. They stabilized him just enough to medi-vac to Miles City, and that's when I figured out, he was fucking dying.

Like… *dying*.

Forty-five minutes later I had a private ambulance pick him up and we flew to Mayo. They were pissed, because I didn't tell them we were coming. If I had, they'd have said no. They will take an emergency case with enough palm greasing, but normally it's a 'no'.

I was not in the mood for 'no'.

There wasn't a chance in hell I was gonna accept a 'no'. Not from anyone.

And when we got there, the doctor said if I had waited another few hours to get him to the hospital and start treatment, Legion would have died.

Died.

Next to me, in bed.

So actually—and this is kinda fucking ironic—the fact that Cash and the sheriff showed up that morning, waking everyone up, causin' a commotion—is the whole reason Legion is still alive.

God is funny. Not really funny. Not at all funny, actually. He just has a way of showing you things you don't wanna see in the most unexpected ways.

His entire body was infected by the time he arrived at Mayo. The wound required surgical debridement, and four high-grade antibiotics failed before the doctors reached for the last-resort: colistin—powerful enough to kill almost anything, toxic enough to risk shutting down his kidneys to do it.

For six days, I sat beside his bed, watching machines breathe for him, praying so hard. Begging for divine intervention.

It worked.

But there was a price.

There's always a price.

Cash thought he was so clever. Get Mercy, get me back to the ranch, problem solved. But he didn't count on Mercy refusing to eat unless she could visit Legion.

Didn't count on me using the Ashby money—*my money, not his*—to hire the best medical team in three states.

Didn't count on me bringing Legion home to recover at the mansion.

I turn away from the window, looking around the circular room. As a child, I used to hide up here when my mother wanted more photos, more poses, more perfect smiles. I'd curl up with books about places I'd never see, people I'd never be.

I never thought I'd be bringing Legion Kane into this house. Not as a guest, not as my... what? Boyfriend seems too small a word for what we are. Too normal. There's nothing normal about us.

Movement catches my eye—a dark spot against the blue sky, growing larger.

The helicopter.

My heart thumps as I press my hands against the glass.

It's really happening. He's coming here.

"Mercy!" I call down the spiral staircase. "It's time! He's here!"

I hear her footsteps pounding through the house, the excited yapping of that ridiculous puppy Cash bought her. Within seconds, she's racing across the lawn, a tiny figure in jeans and a t-shirt, Puddles bounding after her.

But I stay where I am, watching as the helicopter descends toward the helipad near the eastern fence line. From this distance, it looks like a toy, the blades stirring up dust that spirals into the air.

The ambulance is already waiting, just as I arranged. The medical team will bring him to the east wing, to the suite I've had prepared with everything he'll need. A hospital bed, monitoring equipment, IV stands. Private nurses on rotation. Windows that look out over the land that's supposedly mine.

Cash thinks he's won. He thinks bringing Legion here, to Ashby land, somehow proves that the Ashbys always come out on top. That I've chosen my inheritance over Legion.

What he doesn't understand is that he's just given me exactly what I wanted.

Legion and Mercy, both under my roof, where I can protect them.

Where no one can take them from me again.

My brother made a critical mistake. He forced my hand, thinking I'd fold. Instead, he's just revelaed exactly how far I'm willing to go.

The helicopter touches down, and even from this distance, I can see the medical team rushing forward with a stretcher. Mercy stands at the edge of the helipad, held back by one of the security guards, bouncing on her toes.

I should be down there. I should be the first face Legion sees when they bring him off that helicopter. But something keeps me rooted to this spot, watching from above as they load him into the ambulance.

Maybe it's knowing that the moment I walk into that room downstairs, everything changes. Legion won't just be mine anymore—he'll be in Ashby territory. He'll be surrounded by everything he hates, everything he's fought against his whole life.

Or maybe I'm just afraid. Afraid that he'll look at me

differently. Like I've betrayed him somehow, by bringing him here.

The ambulance starts moving slowly up the drive toward the house. Mercy runs alongside it for a few yards before the security guard catches up with her, saying something I can't hear. She nods reluctantly and walks beside him instead, still keeping pace with the vehicle.

I step back from the window, suddenly aware of how I look. I'm wearing one of my old sundresses, my hair pulled back in a simple ponytail. No makeup. Nothing like the woman who stood in the clubhouse wearing Legion's clothes and a fresh tattoo declaring herself his property.

I glance down at my wrist, where the words are still healing, the skin around them pink and slightly raised. PROPERTY OF DEMON.

I haven't covered it up with bracelets because my wrists are ringed with scabbing red marks from where Marcus tied me up and I want Cash to see those marks every time he looks at me.

I want him to burn with shame for what he did. How he helped.

Below, the ambulance pulls up to the east entrance. The medical team jumps out, opening the back doors. The stretcher is wheeled toward the house, surrounded by people in scrubs.

Mercy stands at the door, waiting, holding the puppy in her arms as if for support.

Cash thinks he's won, but he's about to learn that his isn't over.

It's barely begun.

CHAPTER 6
LEGION

The helicopter banks left and my stomach rolls with it. Outside the window, Montana spreads beneath us—patchwork fields, winding rivers, and endless sky.

The nurse beside me checks my IV line. "How are you feeling, Mr. Kane?"

"Like I'm being kidnapped by rich people," I say, not looking at her.

She laughs like I'm joking. I'm not.

The sepsis is gone, but I'm still weak. Three additional days of recovery at Mayo after I woke up, and they still insisted on this whole transport setup. Private medical plane. Helicopter waiting to take me to the Ashby Ranch. I feel like a piece of expensive cargo.

The pilot announces our descent, and my ears pop with the pressure change. Below us, the land shifts from anonymous fields to something I recognize—the familiar contours of Drybone. I can make out the winding ribbon of the dry riverbed that separates Kane land from Ashby territory.

I've never crossed that line before. Not properly. Not through the front door.

The helicopter ride is worse than the plane—louder, shakier, more intimate with the sky. Through the window, I catch my first real look at the Ashby Ranch from above. It's obscene how much land they own, how green it is compared to everything around it. The main house sits in the center like a crown.

Log cabin? Only if ten-thousand square feet of 'rustic' living can count as a cabin.

When we land, the medical team ignores my complaints about the gurney. I argue once, twice, three times before giving up. They've got their procedures. I'm just a body they're transporting.

"I can walk," I tell them for the fourth time as they wheel me out.

"Protocol, Mr. Kane," says the one who seems to be in charge.

Even over the spinning rotors, I can hear her. "Legion! Legion!"

Mercy is running toward the helicopter, her face split with a grin I haven't seen since before I went to prison. Someone catches her before she reaches me—a broad-shouldered man in a black suit, definitely security, not ranch staff. His hand on her shoulder is gentle but firm.

The bodyguard points up at the rotors, tells her something I can't hear. Mercy looks up at the spinning blades, then shrinks back. But when I'm wheeled out from under them, she's there. Rushing up to me, bouncing on her toes, waving frantically. "You look better!" she yells. "Not gray anymore!"

I lift my hand in a small wave, embarrassed by the whole setup—me on a gurney like some invalid, her being held back like I'm dangerous.

No Cash. No Savannah either.

This is a mistake. I should be at the trailer. That double-wide might not feel like home yet, but at least it's mine. Or was. I don't even know if I still have it, or if the club took it back after everything.

They load me into an ambulance for the short drive to the house. Through the back windows, I watch Mercy running alongside until the security guy catches up with her. A small dog yaps at her heels—something fluffy and useless-looking that hasn't had a place in this story of mine until now.

A puppy. Did they have the puppy before Mercy came to live here?

Doubt it.

It's a bribe.

But kids don't care. It's not that Mercy's fallin' for Cash's lies, it's that he's giving her things she could only dream of before now.

Is this what Colt did to Destiny?

I'm not sure. I'm not gonna ask, either. Destiny, young as she is, is an adult now. A mother. She's allowed to make her own mistakes.

Still, it burns. The Ashbys and their money, thinking they can own everything and everyone.

I don't wanna be here. But I'm not leaving Mercy alone with Cash. And there's something deeply satisfying about the thought of Cash having to watch me and Savannah together under his own roof.

Like, as a couple.

In his childhood home.

It almost makes the CPS shit worth it.

Almost.

The ambulance stops and the doors open. Mercy is bouncin' and talkin' like she just drank a hundred Red Bulls.

They pull the gurney out and start to wheel me away, but I grab on to a railing on the ambulance door, and do not let go.

The gurney shifts sideways. Their expressions go sideways too.

I sit up, push my legs over the side, look them in the eyes, and say, "Get the fuck out of my way. Thank you for the help, but I got it from here."

The medic in charge of the transport blows out a breath, figuring he did ninety percent of his job and decides this fight is not worth it. He smiles. "Be my guest." Then moves out of my way.

I stand, shaky, but determined, and look up.

The Ashby mansion is a fuckin' monument to money.

Two stories of logs thick enough to need a crane to lift. Each one stripped and stained the exact same amber-gold. Not a knot out of place. Not a crack showing. The kind of perfect that only comes from paying people to sand away reality.

The roof peaks into what must be fifteen different angles, all covered in slate the color of gunmetal. Chimneys rise from five different spots, though it's too warm for smoke.

The wraparound porch could fit my entire double-wide with room to spare. Cedar pillars thick as tree trunks hold up the overhang, and I count at least four different seating areas with brightly colored cushions. As if people actually sit on the porch in places like this.

Floor-to-ceiling windows line the front, reflecting the Montana sky back at itself. The glass is spotless, probably cleaned daily by servants to make sure the Ashbys don't have to see a single smudge.

"Need help walkin' up?" Mercy asks

"I got it," I tell Mercy, trying to sound upbeat and positive as I ignore the tug of the IV line still feeding antibiotics into my arm. I might be weak, but I'm not an invalid.

Not far off one, either. Which is why it matters. Poor people don't have the luxury of being… whatever this is. Injured, I guess. Incapacitated.

It's the law of the jungle with people like me.

Only the strong get by.

As I walk up the little path, I study the immaculate landscaping. Flower beds burstin' with colors that don't belong in this part of Montana, green grass that must drink a thousand gallons of water a day. Stone pathways branch off toward what looks like a guest house to the left and some kind of pool around the back.

The front door is massive. Ten feet tall, carved with scenes of cattle drives and wild horses. Brass hardware that's polished to a mirror shine. No dust dares settle here.

Beyond the main house, I can see part of the stables

—another perfect structure with copper weather vanes spinning in the breeze. A paddock where three horses graze on grass that's greener than any field that doesn't come with the Ashby name.

That's what so vile about this place. It's not the house. Though it's big enough to be on the gross side of opulent. It's the acres and acres of Ashby territory, stretching toward mountains in the distance.

From here, you can't even see where it ends. That's the real wealth. And the green grass is more of a flex than a whole pile of fuckin' diamonds could ever be. The water rights this one family owns, is sick. The fact that their land stays green when everything else around it burns brown in the summer sun is enough to make me want to turn away and never look at this place again.

"Ready Mr. Kane?" The medic is getting impatient. "We need to get you settled."

I take a step forward, feeling the gravel crunch under my boots that appeared in a package yesterday, along with the jeans and t-shirt I'm wearin' right now.

The front doors swing open before we reach them. A woman in a crisp uniform—not quite a maid, something fancier—nods at me with professional distance.

"Welcome to the Ashby Ranch, Mr. Kane. Miss Ashby is waiting for you inside."

I've never been inside before. Never even been this close to the main house. All those years with Savannah, and we always met at the silo, or by the creek, or in some out of the way place that wasn't on a map.

Now I'm walking through the front door like I belong here.

"Legion." Savannah says my name with a breath of relief. She's waiting for me beneath the towering stone portico entrance, framed by the massive oak columns like some kind of homecoming queen. Her hair is pulled back, face clean of makeup, wearin' a simple sundress that reminds me of the girl she was before college, before Marcus, before everything.

I breathe through the effort it takes to walk over to her and slip my arm around her waist. I don't know the woman who lives in this place. I only know the girl from the silo.

She leans in, cautious, like I might break, and kisses me on the cheek. I turn in to it, take her face in my hands, and kiss her properly.

Her mouth smiles against mine, kissin' me back without hesitation. I didn't do it as a test, but it is one.

Who are we under this roof? Two lovers? Two friends? Two strangers?

"My god, I've missed that tongue of yours." She whispers this into my mouth, answering my unasked question. Then she pulls back a little. "I wish I could take you upstairs, but the doctors say you need to stay on the ground floor. So…" She smiles at me. "I've turned the library into your new bedroom."

The improvised hospital room they've set up is bigger than my entire trailer. Tall windows let in afternoon light, illuminating a space that's been divided into sections—a bedroom area with monitoring equipment, a sitting area with couches, even a dining space. The wet bar in the corner has been converted to a makeshift kitchen.

Mercy talks the entire time they're settling me in, jumping from topic to topic. Her new puppy Puddles. Her bedroom with its own bathroom. The indoor pool in the east wing and the outdoor one out back. There's a chef who makes her whatever she wants for breakfast. And she spends every day in the stables with the horses.

The bribery is so obvious, as is her happiness, my heart goes sad.

"And there's a movie theater downstairs," Mercy says, eyes wide. "With real movie theater seats and popcorn machines."

I don't respond, just watch her bouncin' around the room, looking healthier and happier than I've ever seen her. The guilt sits heavy inside me.

Is this what money does? Turns scared feral kids into happy children?

Yes, Legion. That's exactly what money does.

The medical team leaves after setting up my treatment schedule. I don't have to stay in bed here, which is something at least. They leave the IV port in my arm for the antibiotics I'll need three times a day, but the current treatment is finished and there are no tubes or wires hooked up to anything.

When I'm finally alone with Savannah and Mercy, I pull back the bandage to show them what's left of the brand. The Badlands B is nothin' but wound now. If you squint, and use your imagination, you might still see the shape of a B, but they had to cut away too much dead skin to save it.

"Does it hurt?" Mercy asks, leaning in close.

"Nah." Which is a lie. I can't imagine a time when this brand will ever stop hurtin'. "It just itches now. Feels strange."

Like something foreign is growing under my skin.

Like I'm being unmade.

CHAPTER 7
SAVANNAH

The wealth in this house feels obscene when I think about where Legion came from. Ten days of watching him move through these spaces has been like observing a wild animal in captivity—careful, alert, constantly assessing. When we first brought him in, I caught the flash of disgust across his face before he could hide it. The vaulted ceilings. The hand-carved staircase. The custom stone fireplace that took eight men three months to build.

I saw my home through his eyes for the first time. Not just nice, but oppressive.

By Montana standards, we are the elite of the elite. Most people in Drybone live on the edge of financial collapse, one bad season from bankruptcy. One medical bill from ruin. One drought from selling everything.

But the Ashbys never worry about drought.

I stand at my bedroom window, looking out over our summer pastures—green and lush while the neighboring ranches already show patches of brown. The difference isn't skill or luck.

It's water.

My great-great-great-grandfather bought this land specifically for what lies beneath it—a network of artesian wells that push water to the surface without pumping. While other ranchers drill deeper every year, we have six active wells that never run dry. The paperwork grandfather filed in 1962 secured "first-in-time" water rights that can't be challenged, no matter how desperate the county gets.

The wealth that comes with those rights isn't flashy. It's not diamond necklaces or sports cars. It's the security of knowing your cattle will always drink, your crops will always grow, and your neighbors will always need what you have. In a drought year, those rights are worth more than gold.

I slip a cotton sundress over my head, nothing fancy—just something that will let the summer breeze reach my skin. I've been craving that sensation, wanting to feel alive again after spending so many days in the stale, antiseptic air of Legion's makeshift hospital room.

"Savannah?" Mercy calls from down the hall. "Do you think I can ride Peanut by myself today?"

I smile at her excitement about the pony Cash bought her. I haven't told Legion yet, but Cash mentioned there's an opening at Rimrock Academy outside Glendive—my old day school. The perfect place for a bright kid like Mercy.

Legion will say no, of course. Just because it's Cash offering. But I've seen how Mercy's eyes light up when she talks about the art room and the science lab we toured last week. She'd thrive there.

I push the thought away. That's a battle for another day.

Today is about Legion and me finally getting some time alone. I had to have a careful conversation with Mercy about "grown-up time" yesterday. I've been going absolutely crazy knowing Legion is just downstairs and not up here in my bed. He hasn't been well enough for us to fool around, but after ten days of antibiotics and rest, the color has returned to his face.

Each day has brought visible improvement. That first day, he could barely make it from the ambulance to the front door without pausing to catch his breath. By day three, he was eating full meals on the screened-in back porch, the warm air doing what medicine alone couldn't.

Our walks started as slow shuffles around the garden, then extended to the stables, and yesterday we made it all the way to the creek. His appetite returned first for food, then for conversation, and lately I've caught him watching me with that look that makes my skin feel too tight for my body.

Mercy is still talkin'. I never answered her about riding Peanut, but she doesn't care. That girl talks non-stop these days. She's always got somethin' to say to me. To everyone, really.

I'd never seen Mercy like this. Not that I knew her well, but I did stop by the old trailer on the regular while Legion was inside. She was feral over there.

Here, she's a little ranch princess with a bubbly

personality that can't get enough of what the Ashby Ranch has to offer.

Legion hates it, I can tell.

But he doesn't say anything. Just lets her be.

I head downstairs with Mercy bouncing along in front of me. She's wearing a summer dress I swear could have come straight from my childhood closet, though I have no idea where it came from. The sight makes something twist in my chest—I've never had a little sister before, but I'm starting to understand the appeal.

Legion is already outside on the porch when we arrive, staring out at the mountains with that restless energy I recognize. He's been talking about going home more frequently. Yesterday he mentioned the new trailer twice.

I get it. Cash and Legion circle each other like wolves whenever they're in the same room. Wyatt has mostly kept his distance, staying in one of the guest houses near the river. But I like having Legion here. I want him to stay.

Mercy barely slows down as she passes us. "Hi, Legion! Bye, Legion! Madeline's waiting!"

Cash hired Madeline—my dressage instructor, a former Olympic equestrian—to teach Mercy basic riding. Now this nine-year-old who never had anything gets private lessons from one of the best riders in the world.

The moment Mercy disappears toward the barn, Legion's mouth is on mine. His kiss is hungry, desperate, and wanting, the heat of his body radiating through his clothes as he presses against me. I feel the unmistakable hardness of his arousal against my stomach, his desire for me evident in every taut line of his body.

The intensity of his need sends a shiver down my spine, his hands gripping my waist with a possessiveness that makes my breath catch.

After days of careful distance and restraint during his recovery, this raw, unfiltered passion feels like coming home—dangerous and perfect all at once.

His body remembers what his mind has been forced to deny, and there's no hiding how much he's craved this connection. We've been so careful with his recovery, keeping everything chaste, but his body is clearly done with restraint.

"I have a surprise," I say when we come up for air. "Your antibiotic treatment is officially over. So we're celebratin'."

His eyes darken. "How exactly are we celebratin'?"

I take his hand and lead him toward the driveway where an old Willys Jeep sits loaded with picnic supplies. The vehicle is a faded brown color that reminds me of the sandstone cliffs near Drybone. And though it's a ranch vehicle—a favorite of the ranch hands—there's no logo on it.

"Want to drive?" I ask, holding up the keys.

Legion's face breaks into a genuine smile as he runs his hand along the hood, his fingers tracing the weathered metal with reverence. "This thing is a classic," he says, eyes lighting up with appreciation for the vintage military vehicle before us.

He looks so much better than he did ten days ago. The white t-shirt stretches across shoulders that have regained their strength. His faded jeans hang perfectly on his hips. He looks so good now, you'd almost never know he was on death's door three weeks ago.

Only I know about the scars hiding underneath—the healing tissue where his brand was, the marks from prison, the story of his life written on his skin.

We climb in, the Jeep's engine roaring to life with Legion behind the wheel. I direct him away from the main house, past the eastern pastures where the tall grasses sway in the afternoon breeze, and toward a secluded canyon formation I've known since childhood—a place where the sandstone walls rise up like ancient guardians, their surfaces etched with decades of wind and weather.

The dirt path narrows as we approach, winding between juniper trees and scrubby sagebrush that release their earthy scent with each step.

We park the Willys at the trailhead, its engine ticking as it cools in the summer heat. I gather our supplies from the back—Legion hefting the heavy wicker picnic basket with one hand as if it weighs nothing, the muscles in his forearm flexing beneath his tattoos. I take the soft cotton blankets, their edges worn from countless family outings, though this is the first time I've brought anyone here aside from Colt.

The way Legion's eyes scan the landscape, taking in every detail, makes me wonder if he's memorizing an escape route, or simply appreciating the wild beauty that's always been my sanctuary.

The canyon isn't far, just enough of a walk to feel like we've earned our privacy. It's a natural alcove carved into the sandstone, sheltered from prying eyes by an overhanging lip of rock that curves like a protective hand above us. The weathered formation creates a perfect pocket of seclusion—a secret chamber that feels both exposed to the elements, and completely hidden from the world.

Centuries of wind and water have hollowed out this sanctuary, sculpting the warm amber stone into a space that seems designed specifically for forbidden love.

The ground beneath our feet is almost powdery, fine particles of eroded stone create a soft, sand-like cushion against the hard earth.

The sun's direct rays can't penetrate this hidden pocket, creating a cool refuge from the relentless summer heat that bakes the plains beyond. Wind has sculpted the interior walls into smooth, undulating curves that seem to embrace us as we step deeper into the shadow. And the air feels different here—still and ancient, carrying the faint mineral scent of stone.

We spread the blankets over the soft ground. I've barely straightened the last corner when Legion's hands are on my waist, turning me to face him.

"I've been thinking about this for days," he says, his voice rough with desire, the words catching in his throat like they've been waiting too long to escape. His eyes lock with mine, dark with hunger and something deeper—a need that's been building steadily over the past ten days. "It's been agony knowin' you're upstairs and I can't go up because of that stupid rule."

He gives me a side-eye, which makes me giggle.

He tried to climb the steps on day four, but was stopped by a servant. "No guests upstairs," the housekeeper, Eileen, told him. And older woman who's been working for us since she was nineteen. She wagged a finger at him. "Never. Ever. Ever."

Legion backed off and didn't try again.

"But now," Legion continues, "I've got you all to myself." His fingers trace the curve of my jaw, callused skin against softness, leaving trails of fire wherever he touches.

His mouth finds mine again, and this time there's no holding back. His tongue slides against mine as his hands grip my hips, pulling me against him. I can feel how much he wants me, his cock hard and insistent through his jeans.

God, I've dreamed about this every night he was downstairs, imagining his hands on me again, wondering if he was lying awake thinking the same things.

"Missed you," I whisper against his mouth. "Missed this."

Legion lowers me onto the blanket, his body covering mine. His weight feels perfect, solid and real after so many nights of sleeping alone while he recovered downstairs. He kisses down my neck, his breath hot against my skin as his hand slides up my thigh, pushing my dress higher.

"Where are your fuckin' panties?" he growls when his fingers find bare skin.

I smile up at him. "Ooops," I giggle. "I guess I forgot them."

"You're bad."

"You make me bad. But don't worry, I'm only bad with you." I place my fingertip on his lips, letting them part slightly to lick, then trace his mouth. He bites my fingertip, being deliberately gentle. Using his tongue to play with it. Swirling around the sensitive pad.

The wet heat of his mouth sends electric currents racing through my body, igniting nerves I'd forgotten existed during our time apart. And the intensity in those blue eyes of his make me shiver—like he's reading every secret I've ever kept, every thought I've hidden away.

His stare penetrates deeper than touch ever could, seeing through the carefully constructed layers of Savannah Ashby to the raw, wanting woman beneath.

"Legion," I breathe, my hands moving to his belt. "I need you." His fingers trace the curve of my hip, pushing my dress higher with deliberate slowness. His eyes never leave mine as he reveals me inch by inch, like he's unwrapping something precious and forbidden all at once.

"You planned this," he says, voice rough with want. "Coming out here where no one can hear you scream my name."

I bite my lip, not denying it. "Of course, I did. I'm dying for you, Legion. It took every ounce of self-control not to press my vibrator against my pussy, knowin' you're downstairs."

He chuckles. "So you've got pent-up frustration?"

"You have no idea."

His hand slides between my thighs, fingers brushing against me with feather light pressure. Just enough to make me arch up, seeking more. "So wet already," he murmurs, satisfaction darkening his voice. "Do you promise you've been a good girl? That you've kept your fingers and your toy away from my pussy?"

"I promise," I say, my breath catching as his thumb circles my clit. "I can't pleasure myself knowin' you're so close and you can do it so much better."

Legion tilts his head to the side, blue eyes still locked with mine, as he pushes a finger inside me. I gasp.

"Like this?" he asks, curling his finger in a way that makes my hips buck against his hand. "Do you never touch yourself like this, thinking about me? Never, Savannah? Tell me the truth."

"I do. When you were gone, I did it a lot," I whisper, heat flooding my cheeks even as my body responds to his touch. "But it's not the same."

He adds a second finger, stretching me deliciously as his thumb continues its maddening circles. "Tell me," he demands, his voice dropping lower. "Tell me what you think about when you're fingering yourself."

The intensity in his eyes makes it impossible to look away, impossible to hide. "Your mouth," I admit. "Your tongue on my pussy. Your hands. The way they grab my tits. The way your cock feels inside me."

Legion's smile is pure sin. "Show me your tits," he commands, his fingers still working between my legs.

I reach down and pull my dress up higher, exposing my breasts to the open air. Legion's eyes darken as he takes in the sight, his fingers momentarily stilling inside me.

"Fuck, you're so perfect," he groans, lowering his head to take one nipple into his mouth.

The wet heat of his tongue sends lightning through my body. I arch up, pressing myself more firmly against his mouth as his fingers resume their rhythm inside me.

He sucks hard, then releases my nipple, moving to the other one, giving it the same attention.

"Legion," I gasp, my hands clutching at his shoulders. "Please."

He lifts his head, his eyes meeting mine again. "Please what, princess?" he asks, curling his fingers in that way that makes me see stars. "Tell me what you need."

"You," I manage, my voice breaking as his thumb presses harder against my clit. "Inside me. Now."

Legion shakes his head slowly, his fingers continuing their relentless pace. "Not yet. I want to watch you come apart for me first."

His mouth returns to my breast, teeth grazing my nipple as his fingers thrust deeper. The dual sensation is overwhelming, pleasure building at the base of my spine like a gathering storm.

"That's it," he murmurs against my skin. "Let go for me, baby."

I'm close, so close, my body trembling on the edge. Legion senses it, his fingers moving faster, harder, his mouth hot and demanding on my breast.

"Legion," I cry out, my back arching as the first waves of pleasure crash through me. "Oh God, Legion!"

He doesn't slow down, working me through the orgasm, drawing it out until I'm shaking and incoherent beneath him. Only then does he withdraw his fingers, bringing them to his mouth to taste me as I watch through half-lidded eyes.

"Fucking delicious," he says, his voice thick with need. "Ready for more?"

CHAPTER 8
LEGION

I stand up so I can see her properly. Savannah is breathing hard, all stretched out on the blanket with her legs open and her dress pulled up to her chin. It's a dirty fuckin' pose, but the sunlight catches on the sweat beading on her skin, turning her into somethin' golden.

"Take off the dress," I tell her, my voice thick with everything I'm trying not to say. "Do it slow, so I can enjoy it."

Savannah smiles, that same goddamn smile that's been haunting me since I was fourteen. Not the perfect Ashby heiress smile she gives to cameras, but the one that lives in the corners of her mouth when she knows she's got me by the throat.

"Yes, sir," she whispers, drawing out the words like she's tasting them.

She sits up, angling her legs into a side pose, her hair falling across her shoulders in waves. The movement shifts her breasts, and I clench my fists at my sides to keep from grabbing her. Patience has never been my strong suit, but with Savannah, I've learned to savor the wait.

Her fingers find the bunched fabric at her neck. She slides the dress up, inch by slow inch, revealing her face like she's emerging from water. When it's off, she shakes out her hair, letting it fall wild around her shoulders.

"Better?" she asks, tossing the dress aside.

"Much."

Then she does something that stops my breath. She looks right at me, those blue eyes burning into mine, and slowly spreads her legs open. The pink flesh between her thighs glistens wet, already slick for me. I swallow hard at the sight, transfixed by that perfect V, the soft folds parting like she's offering up a secret only I'm allowed to know.

She doesn't look away, doesn't blink, just holds my gaze.

My cock goes rock hard instantly, straining against my jeans. Blood rushes south so fast I feel dizzy with it. I want her so fucking bad my hands shake when I reach for my belt buckle. The metal clinks as I work it open, then pop the button on my jeans. I lower the zipper tooth by tooth, watching her watch me.

For a moment, I stand over her, letting her eyes linger on the bulge beneath my jeans. Her lips part slightly, her tongue darting out to wet them. I watch her watching me, savoring the hunger in her eyes.

My hand trembles slightly as I pull my cock free, wrapping my fingers around the base. I begin to stroke slowly, deliberately, from root to tip, letting her see exactly what she does to me.

Savannah watches me as I jerk off, her eyes following every stroke, every twist of my wrist with a hunger that burns hotter than the summer air around us. Her gaze tracks the movement of my hand with such raw intensity it feels like she's memorizing every detail. The way she looks at me—like I'm something sacred and sinful all at once—makes my cock throb harder in my grip.

I drop to my knees, leaning back as I continue to masturbate. "Touch yourself," I tell her, my voice dropping to that dangerous register that makes her pupils dilate. "I want to watch you play with that pretty pussy while I jerk off. Show me how you like it when I'm not there."

Her cheeks flush a deep rose that spreads down her neck. But it's not embarrassment. It's arousal. With a slowness that feels deliberate, her hand glides down the flat plane of her stomach, fingers trailing a path of goosebumps before disappearing between her creamy thighs.

When she makes contact with her wet pussy, a soft gasp escapes her lips. Her eyelids fluttering closed momentarily—just long enough for her to absorb the first wave of pleasure—before they snap back open to lock with mine.

Our breathing synchronizes into a ragged, primal rhythm, chests rising and falling unevenly as we devour each other with our eyes. Both performers and audience, as we bathe in the dusty afternoon light.

"You're so fucking beautiful," I say, my voice rough. "Look at that perfect pussy. Pink and wet and glistening in the light. Practically begging for me to taste it, and claim it as mine. To feel it pulse around my cock as you come apart."

Her fingers move faster, circling her clit. Her other hand slides up to cup her breast, pinching her nipple between her fingers.

"Is this what you do when you're alone?" I ask, squeezing my cock harder as I stroke. "Think about me while you touch yourself?"

"Yes," she breathes, her hips lifting slightly off the blanket, muscles tensing as her fingers work faster. "Always you, Legion. Every single time. Nobody else. Just you." Her voice breaks into a soft whimper as she arches her back, golden hair spilling across the worn fabric beneath her like liquid sunlight.

I kick off my boots, pushing them aside without looking. Then I peel my jeans down my legs, stepping out of them. I stand before her completely naked, hand still wrapped around my cock, working it slowly.

"Your cock is so fucking massive," she whispers, her eyes locked on my hand as I continue stroking myself. Her voice drops even lower, husky with desire. "I love how it stretches me wide open every time. How it reaches places inside me nobody else has ever touched. How it makes me feel so completely full I can barely breathe when you're buried all the way inside me."

Fuck, her dirty talk drives me nuts. Always has. It was a surprise how filthy her fuckin' mouth was that first time when we were teenagers. She's never been shy. I said one dirty thing to her that first time. Told her she was wet, or something stupid like that. And the filthy words I got in response almost killed me. Something about ruined panties.

I drop to my knees between her spread legs, pushin' them wider with my hands. I lower my mouth to her pussy, breathing in her scent before my tongue makes contact with her slick flesh. The taste of her floods my mouth, sweet and tangy and perfect.

I lick a long, deliberate stripe from her entrance to her clit, savoring the sweet tang of her arousal as it coats my tongue. She responds immediately. Her thighs quiverin' against my shoulders.

I take my time eating her out, letting my tongue press firm and flat against her opening. Then dragging slowly upward until I reach her swollen clit.

"Fuck, Legion," she moans, her back arching off the blanket.

I circle her clit with my tongue, applying just enough pressure to make her squirm but not enough to push her over the edge. I want to draw this out, make her beg for it. I slip two fingers inside her, bending them upward to make her see stars.

Savannah writhes beneath me, her hips bucking against my face. Her hands tangle in my hair, trying to pull me up to her, but I resist. I love doing this to her, watching her come apart under my mouth. The power of it, knowing I can reduce her to nothin' but desperate need with just my tongue and fingers.

"Legion, please," she gasps, tugging harder at my hair. "I want your cock inside me. I need you to fuck me right now. I've been thinking about it for days, watching you in that bed, wanting to climb on top of you, but knowing I couldn't."

I lift my head, my lips and chin wet with her. "You want my cock, princess? You want me to fill up this tight little pussy until you can't remember your own name? I'm going to fuck you so deep you'll feel me for days. Every time you sit down, you'll remember how I stretched you open, how I claimed every inch of you. This pussy belongs to me, Savannah. No one else gets to touch it, taste it, fuck it. Just me."

My fingers work faster inside her. Her walls clench around them, telling me she's close.

"Your pussy gets so wet for me," I continue, my voice low and dark. "So fucking wet and ready. I love watching you fall apart like this, knowing that I'm the only one who gets to see the Ashby princess begging for cock. You're mine, Savannah. Every perfect inch of you belongs to me now. I'm going to fuck you until you can't walk straight, until all you can think about is when you'll get my cock again."

"Yes," she moans, her head thrashing from side to side. "I'm yours, Legion. Only yours. Please, I need you inside me now."

I can't deny her any longer. I slide between her legs, positioning the head of my cock at her entrance. I push forward slowly, watching her face as I fill her inch by inch. Her mouth falls open in a silent gasp, her eyes locked on mine as I sink into her completely.

"Fuck," I groan, stilling once I'm fully seated inside her. "So tight. So perfect."

Everything that's happened since I got out of prison flashes through my mind—Savannah's engagement, the beatings, the infection, nearly dying, the club turning its back on me. My life is a complete shit show, but none of it matters as long as Savannah is mine. As long as I can bury myself inside her like this, feel her heart beating against mine, I don't care what else happens.

I lower my head to her breast, taking a nipple into my mouth. I suck hard, then graze it with my teeth, feeling her pussy clench around me in response. I move to the other breast, giving it the same attention while my hips begin a slow, deep rhythm.

"Roll over," I tell her, my voice rough with desire, pulling out just long enough for us to switch positions. The cool air hits my cock and I'm desperate to be inside her again.

Savannah is down on all fours, presenting herself to me, her perfect ass raised in invitation. I take a moment to appreciate the view, running my hands over the curve of her hips as I align myself with wet pussy.

I tease her first, sliding the length of my cock between her legs, feeling her tremble with anticipation. Leaning forward, I drape my body over hers, my chest pressed to her back, my lips grazing the nape of her neck. I feel her skin pebble beneath my breath, goosebumps cascading down her spine as she arches into me.

Then I lean back and spread her cheeks with my hands, my thumb brushing over her tight entrance. The thought crosses my mind, to fuck her in the ass—one day, maybe, but not now. Not today.

My focus narrows to the pink pussy between her thighs. I press my cock forward and she backs her ass into it. I enter her moaning, gripping her hips so hard, I make her hiss. But she doesn't stop me. Just moans, "Fuck me, Legion, do it now."

I thrust forward, desperate now, needing to be

inside her so goddamn bad it's almost painful. The sensation of her tight pussy wrapping around my cock makes me groan—something primal and raw that comes from deep in my chest.

"Fuck yes," I breathe, gripping her hips tighter as I pull back and drive forward again, harder this time.

Savannah meets me thrust for thrust, banging her ass backward into my hips each time I push forward. The sound of our bodies colliding fills the canyon—skin slapping against skin, wet and obscene and perfect.

"Yes," I say, my eyes locked on where we're joined. Watching my cock slide in and out of her pussy, glistening with her wetness. "Look at you, taking every inch like you were made for it."

Her tits rock back and forth with each thrust, swaying beneath her as her fingers grip the blanket so tight her knuckles turn white. Sounds start comin' out of her mouth now that will make me hard just thinkin' about them tomorrow—high, breathy whimpers that turn into moans, then into something closer to screams.

"Harder," she gasps, her voice breaking. "Fuck me harder, Legion."

I give her what she wants, what she's begging for. I pull almost all the way out, then slam back inside her so deep I feel her whole body jolt forward. She cries out, her back arching as she pushes back against me, demanding more.

"That's my girl," I growl, setting a brutal pace now. "Taking my cock so fucking well. You love this, don't you? Love getting fucked like this where anyone could see."

"God, yes," she moans, her voice muffled as she

drops her head between her arms. "I love it. I love your cock. I love how you fuck me."

The sight of her like this—the perfect Ashby princess on her hands and knees, taking every inch I give her—sends something dark and possessive through me. This is mine. She is mine. Not Cash's sister, not Marcus's ex-fiancée, not Eleanor's daughter.

Mine.

"Say it," I demand, my fingers digging into the soft flesh of her hips hard enough to leave marks. "Tell me who you belong to."

"You," she gasps immediately, her pussy clenching around me. "I belong to you, Legion. Only you."

"Damn right," I grunt, reaching forward to grab a fistful of her hair. I pull her head back, arching her spine, changing the angle so I'm hitting that spot inside her that makes her see stars. "This pussy is mine. This body is mine. All of you is mine."

"Yes, yes, yes," she chants, her voice climbing higher with each word.

I can feel her getting close, her walls starting to flutter around my cock. My own release is building at the base of my spine, hot and insistent, but I want her to come first. Need to feel her fall apart on my cock before I let myself go.

I release her hair and reach around to find her clit, circling it with my fingers while I continue fucking her hard and deep. Her whole body tenses, every muscle going taut as a bowstring.

"Come for me," I order, my voice rough. "Come on my cock, Savannah. Let me feel it."

Her response is immediate and devastating. She

screams my name as her orgasm crashes through her, her pussy clamping down on my cock so tight I almost lose control right then.

I keep fucking her through it, maintaining that punishing rhythm even as her legs shake and her arms threaten to give out. Every thrust pulls another cry from her lips, another flutter of her walls around me. Her whole body is trembling now, overwhelmed by sensation, caught in that beautiful space between pleasure and too much.

"That's it," I rasp, my voice barely recognizable. "Give me everything."

She does. Wave after wave of her climax rolls through her, each one making her clench around me, making her gasp my name like I'm the only thing keeping her tethered to earth. I don't let up, don't slow down, fucking her through every aftershock until she's gasping and trembling beneath me, completely wrecked.

I'm wrecked too. And I want to blow inside her.

But not in her pussy.

I pull out fast, my cock slick and throbbing. The cool air hits me like a shock after the wet heat of her pussy. I'm so close to coming I can barely think straight, but I want this—need this—her mouth on me when I finally let go.

I grab a fistful of her hair, not gentle, and guide her around to face me. My cock bobs between us, angry red and dripping with her wetness.

Savannah looks up at me—those blue eyes wide with surprise at the sudden movement. Her lips are parted, breath coming fast. Sweat gleams on her skin, her hair a tangled mess from my hands. She's never looked more beautiful.

For a moment, I wonder if she'll object. If this is too much, too dirty, even for us.

But then she smiles, slow and wicked, and her hands come up to grip my cock tight. Both of them wrapped around me, squeezing.

"That's it," I tell her, my voice barely more than a growl. "Take my dick. Rip me apart. Put my come wherever you want it."

She doesn't hesitate. Her tongue darts out, licking the head of my cock, tasting herself on me. The sensation nearly buckles my knees. I tighten my grip in her hair, using it to steady myself as much as to control her.

"Fuck," I breathe, watching her pink tongue swirl around the tip, lapping up the precum that's been leaking since I pulled out of her.

She looks up at me while she does it, holding my gaze with those innocent-looking eyes that are anything but. Then she opens her mouth wider and takes me inside. Just the head at first, her lips forming a perfect seal around me as she sucks.

My vision goes hazy at the edges. The wet heat of her mouth, the gentle scrape of her teeth, the way her tongue works the underside of my cock—it's almost too much to handle after fucking her so hard. I'm already so close, wound so tight, that I know this won't last long.

"More," I rasp, my hand in her hair urging her forward. "Take more of me."

Savannah complies, sliding down my length inch by inch. I watch my cock disappear between those perfect lips, watch her throat work as she takes me deeper. When she gags slightly, I feel it all along my shaft—a flutter, a squeeze that makes my balls draw up tight.

"That's my good girl," I murmur, fightin' to keep my eyes open, to watch every second of this. "Taking that cock so well. So fucking perfect."

She moans around me, the vibration traveling straight through my body. Her hands move to my hips, gripping tight as she starts to bob her head, creating a rhythm that's going to destroy me. Slow at first, then faster, her cheeks hollowing as she sucks harder.

I let her set the pace for a minute, just savorin' the sight of the Little Ashby Princess on her knees in front of me, my cock buried in her throat. But then the need to take control, to claim her completely, overwhelms me.

I tighten my grip in her hair and start to move her head myself, fuckin' her mouth with shallow thrusts at first. Testin'. She relaxes her jaw, opens wider, lets me use her however I want. The trust in that gesture, the complete surrender, makes something fierce and possessive roar to life in my chest.

"Fuck, Savannah," I groan, my hips snapping forward harder now. "Your mouth feels so goddamn good. So wet and perfect wrapped around my cock."

Tears form at the corners of her eyes from the effort, from taking me so deep, but she doesn't pull away. Doesn't even slow down. Just keeps looking up at me with those watery blue eyes, letting me see exactly what I'm doing to her.

The pressure at the base of my spine builds to a breaking point. My thrusts become erratic, desperate. I can feel my release coming, inevitable and powerful, building like a wave about to crash.

"I'm gonna come," I warn her, my voice rough and strained. "Gonna fill that pretty mouth with my cum. You want that? Want me to come down your throat?"

She moans her agreement, the sound muffled by my cock, and that's it. That's all it takes to send me over the edge.

My orgasm slams into me with brutal force. I hold her head in place as I come, my cock pulsing as I empty myself into her mouth. Wave after wave of release, so intense my vision goes white at the edges. I can feel her swallowing, her throat working around me, taking everything I give her.

"Fuck, fuck, fuck," I chant, the words punctuated by each spasm of pleasure.

When it finally subsides, when I've given her everything I have, I slowly release my grip on her hair. My legs feel weak, my whole body trembling from the intensity of it.

Savannah pulls back, my cock slipping from her lips with an obscene wet sound. She looks up at me, her makeup smeared, her lips swollen and red, a drop of my cum glistening at the corner of her mouth. She licks it away, slow and deliberate, never breaking eye contact.

"Good?" she asks, her voice husky.

I can't form words. Can barely remember my own name. My whole body feels like it's been cracked open and put back together wrong—or maybe right for the first time in my life.

So I just nod, dropping down beside her feet. The

blanket is soft beneath my back, still warm from where we were just tangled together. I reach for her, my hands finding her waist, pulling her on top of me.

"More?" she asks, half laughing as she straddles me. Her wet pussy settles against my shaft, cradling it, and I feel her heat even through the haze of my exhaustion.

But then she looks down. Her eyes widen slightly as she realizes what I already know.

I'm still rock hard.

My cock throbs between us, still slick from her mouth, from her pussy, refusing to soften despite the fact that I just came so hard I saw stars. It's like my body knows something my mind hasn't caught up to yet—that I'll never get enough of her. That I could fuck her a hundred times and still want more.

I take her face in my hands. Force her to look at me, hold those blue eyes with mine.

"Yes, Savannah," I rasp, my voice still rough from groaning her name. "More."

Her breath catches. I feel it, see the way her pupils dilate.

"Ride me now," I tell her, my thumbs stroking her cheekbones. "Ride me slow. Fuck me good, just like I did you."

For a moment, she just stares at me. Her hair falls around us like a curtain, blocking out the rest of the world. It's just us in this canyon alcove—just her blue eyes and my hands on her face and the pulse of want between us that won't quit.

Then she shifts her hips, reaches down between us, and wraps her fingers around my cock.

The touch sends electricity straight up my spine. I'm

so sensitive after coming, every nerve ending raw and exposed, that just her hand on me feels like too much and not nearly enough.

She positions me at her entrance. I can feel how wet she still is, how ready. My hands fall from her face to her hips, gripping tight as she starts to sink down onto me.

Slow. So fucking slow.

Inch by inch, her pussy opens around me, taking me inside. The drag of her walls against my oversensitive cock is almost painful in its intensity. I grit my teeth, my fingers digging into her flesh hard enough to bruise.

"Fuck," I breathe, watching her face as she takes me. Watching the way her eyes flutter closed, the way her mouth falls open on a silent gasp.

She doesn't stop until I'm buried completely inside her, until she's sitting on my lap with my cock as deep as it can go. Then she pauses, adjusting to the fullness, her hands braced on my chest for balance.

I can feel her pulse where we're joined. Can feel the slight tremor in her thighs, the way her whole body is wound tight with renewed desire despite the fact that I already made her come so hard she screamed.

"Look at me," I order, my voice low and rough.

Her eyes open, locking onto mine. There's something wild in them now, something unleashed. The perfect Ashby princess is gone. This is just Savannah—raw and real and mine.

"Ride," I tell her.

She does.

Lifting herself up slowly, almost all the way off my cock, before sliding back down just as deliberately.

Setting a rhythm that's designed to torture us both—slow and deep and devastating. Each movement deliberate, controlled, wringing every sensation from both our bodies.

I watch her move above me. Watch the way her tits bounce with each roll of her hips. Watch the late afternoon sun catch in her blonde hair, turning it gold. Watch the way pleasure transforms her face—lips parted, eyes half-closed, a flush spreading down her neck to her chest.

My hands roam from her hips to her waist to her breasts, unable to settle on just one part of her when I want all of it. When I want to touch every inch of her at once, mark her, claim her, make sure she knows exactly who she belongs to.

"That's it," I murmur, my thumbs finding her nipples, circling them until they're hard peaks. "Take what you need. Use my cock however you want it."

She moans at my words, her rhythm faltering slightly. Her hands slide up my chest, fingers tracing over the tattooed angels and demons, careful around the still-healing brand. The touch is reverent, possessive, claiming me just as surely as I've claimed her.

"Legion," she breathes, my name falling from her lips like a prayer.

"I'm right here," I tell her, one hand moving to where we're joined, my thumb finding her clit. "Right here with you."

Savannah closes her eyes, drops her head back, exposing her throat. The line of it stretches pale and perfect in the fading light—vulnerable, trusting, completely open to me.

One hand goes up. Mine. I don't even think about it, don't plan the movement. My fingers just wrap around her throat, spannin' the delicate column, feeling her pulse jump beneath my palm.

Her eyes fly open, wide and startled. Blue meeting mine with something like shock, like she didn't expect this even though she offered herself up for it.

"It's okay," I soothe, my thumb stroking the side of her neck. Gentle. Reverent. "Don't worry. I won't press hard. I'll be gentle. Just... fuck me, Savannah. Just fuck me."

Her breath comes faster. I feel it against my palm, feel the way her throat works as she swallows. The vulnerability of the moment settles between us like somethin' sacred. She's still riding me, her hips rolling slow and deliberate, her pussy squeezing my cock with each movement.

But now there's this—my hand on her throat. Not choking, not threatening. Just holding. Claiming. A reminder that she's mine and I'm hers and there's nothin' between us anymore except skin and sweat and this desperate need that won't quit.

"Trust me," I murmur, my other hand still working her clit in slow circles.

She does. I see it in her eyes—the moment she lets go of the surprise, the fear, and just surrenders to it. Her body relaxes above me, her hips picking up speed, riding me harder now. Using my cock exactly how she needs it.

My fingers stay loose around her throat. Light

enough that she could pull away if she wanted. Firm enough that she knows I'm there, knows I've got her. The pulse beneath my palm pounds faster, matching the rhythm of her movements.

"That's it," I rasp. "Take it. Take what's yours."

She moans, her head still tilted back, giving me her throat completely. The trust in that gesture makes somethin' fierce and protective surge through my chest. This woman—this perfect, maddening, beautiful woman—chose me. Chose this. Chose all the darkness and demons that come with loving Legion Kane.

Her pace quickens. I can feel her getting close again, her walls starting to flutter around my cock. The hand on her throat feels her breathing change—shorter, sharper, desperate.

"You gonna come again?" I ask, my voice rough. "Gonna come on my cock while I hold this pretty throat?"

"Yes," she gasps. "Yes, Legion, please—"

I don't make her beg. Don't make her wait. My thumb presses harder on her clit, circling faster, and the fingers around her throat tighten just slightly—not enough to restrict, just enough to remind her who's holding her, who's got her, who she belongs to.

She shatters. Her whole body goes taut, her back arching, throat pressing harder into my palm as her orgasm crashes through her. The sound she makes is broken and raw, my name torn from her lips like a confession. Her pussy clamps down on my cock so hard it borders on painful, milking me, demanding everything I have left.

The sight of her coming undone destroys me.

I blow inside her pussy like hellfire, sudden, and brutal, and inevitable. My hips buck up hard, driving deeper into her as my cock pulses, spilling my come inside her. Hot and thick and endless. Wave after wave of it filling her pussy while she's still trembling through the aftershocks of her own release.

"Savannah," I breathe, her name a prayer on my lips as my come leaks down the side of my cock, dripping out of her. There's a mark on her neck. Not a bruise, just a faint outline of where my hand was.

Savannah… her names echoes in my head.

She is all I've ever wanted.

She is all I'll ever need.

CHAPTER 9
SAVANNAH

I collapse against Legion's chest, my breathing still ragged, my body limp with satisfaction. The sun plays hide-and-seek behind the banded claystone walls of our canyon hideaway, casting shifting patterns across our tangled bodies.

This little alcove has been my secret place since childhood—a natural fortress of rock where even my mother's camera couldn't find me.

Now it's ours.

Legion's heartbeat thumps steady beneath my ear. His fingers thread through my hair, separating the strands with gentle precision. Neither of us speaks. We don't need to.

I trace the edge of his brand with my fingertip. The infection has receded, leaving behind a mess of scar tissue—angry and red, but healing. Ten days of antibiotics and around-the-clock care have pulled him back from the edge. The memory of his fever-bright eyes and incoherent mumbling still wakes me at night, cold sweat prickling my skin.

I want this silence to last forever. I want this peace we find ourselves in, to be real.

But it's not and so... eventually... the words come.

And they come from him, not me.

Because this can't last.

"So..." Legion starts, his voice vibrating through his chest and into my ear. "What's the plan?"

What's the plan. I could ask what he means, but why? I know what he's asking. What's the plan for us? Because it sure as hell isn't living on my family ranch like the Ashby's and Kanes are just some big happy family.

I don't want to talk about this. Not now. Not when his skin is still warm against mine, not when I can still feel the phantom thickness of his cock inside me.

Instead of answering, I turn over and hook my leg across his hip. I press my lips to the side of his neck, just below his jaw where his pulse beats strong and steady. My fingertips trace down his stomach, barely touching, following the trail of blonde hair that disappears beneath the blanket.

I find him. Not fully hard again, but getting there.

Legion chuckles, but puts a hand on mine to stop the intervention.

"What's wrong?" I murmur, my words low and soft as they touch his ear. "Did I wear you out? Is the Little Ashby Princess too much for big bad Demon Kane?"

Legion smiles. He knows I'm changing the subject, but if he cares, he doesn't show it. Instead, he places his hands behind his head and lets me play with him. I wrap my fingers around his shaft, stroking him casually —not trying to have sex again, just enjoying the feel of him growing harder under my touch. Just enjoying the fact that he's mine.

For the first time in my life, I've got Legion Kane all to myself.

Is it a crime that I want to enjoy it?

"I love you," I whisper against his collarbone, the words muffled but unmistakable.

His fingers begin a gentle exploration of my hair, separating the strands, twisting them around his fingers before letting them fall.

"I feel so much better," Legion says, breaking the spell I'm tryin' to put him under. His hand slides from my hair to my bare shoulder, tracing lazy patterns on my skin. "Thank you for everything you've done, Savannah. The medical team, bringing me here, taking care of Mercy. I don't know what would've happened if—"

Something cold slips into my stomach despite the warmth of the sun on my back.

He's better now.

He can leave.

I've been so focused on getting him well that I haven't let myself think about what happens after. But the truth crashes down on me all at once.

Legion never had any plans to stay at the ranch.

It was only ever a necessity—for his health, for Mercy's safety.

A temporary solution to an immediate problem.

Neither of us says anything, at least, not out loud. But Legion's eyes shift from mine to some point over my shoulder, and that's all the confirmation I need. There's nowhere for him to go but the new trailer and the club. I'm probably welcome at the club, seeing as I did get claimed—the fresh tattoo on my wrist healed now.

But Mercy isn't. It's not a place for children.

Even if Legion and I leave together, Mercy isn't going anywhere. The court gave temporary custody to Cash.

Legion knows this.

I don't want to bring it up. None of this was Legion's fault. It was all Cash's doing, his twisted idea of getting even with... well, with the world probably. With Legion specifically. With me for choosing Legion. With Colt for getting Destiny pregnant.

Cash and I haven't talked about baby Marigold yet. We've been circling each other in the house like wary animals, both of us pretending the other doesn't exist. But that baby is a huge factor in why Mercy is living at the ranch now.

Cash's ideas about revenge run deep, and this situation is the perfect storm for his particular brand of vindictiveness.

First, his little sister gets swept off her feet by an outlaw biker.

Then his brother goes and has an illegitimate child with the outlaw's middle sister.

The symmetry must drive Cash absolutely insane.

The Ashby and Kane families are good and twisted up now. And that's only the beginning. The birth of baby Marigold changes the line of inheritance in ways none of us understand yet. Cash has called in a whole team of lawyers trying to figure out the complicated legalese in Eleanor's will, but there are several interpretations as to what the addition of a female grandbaby means.

Legion's eyes drift back to mine, something changing in his expression. He sighs, reading my thoughts like they're printed across my forehead.

"I know what you're thinking," he says, voice dropping lower. "And you're right. I've got nothing to offer you except my love and my loyalty. I know that's not much compared to all this." He gestures vaguely at the walls of our little canyon, but is really talkin' about the ranch itself. "But I'm rising up in the club. I've earned my place there. I've paid for it in blood and time."

He sits up straighter, warming to his topic, conviction building with each word.

"We could stay at the trailer. It's not much, but it's mine. It's clean. It's safe. I know it's beneath you—"

"Stop." I cut him off, feeling a flush of heat that isn't entirely desire. "That's insulting, Legion."

His eyebrows shoot up.

"I'm more than happy to live at the trailer," I continue, sitting up and reaching for my dress. "It's beautiful. And it's yours. That's what matters to me."

The tension in his shoulders ease, and a smile—small but genuine—touches his lips.

"So that's settled then." He nods once, like we've just signed a contract.

But nothing's settled. Not really.

"Legion, you don't understand what's happening with Mercy. This custody thing is real. Cash isn't just letting her stay with us temporarily. He's filing for permanent custody."

Legion stares at me, his face hardening.

"He's secured a place for her at Rimrock Academy," I add. "My old day school."

"What the fuck?" Legion pushes me off him, standing abruptly. Immediately, he is pulling his jeans up over his hips. "He's got no right—"

"He thinks he does," I say, rising to stand beside him. I pick up my dress, pull it over my head. "And the courts might agree." I place my hand on his cheek, feeling the muscles tense beneath my palm. "Why is Rimrock such a bad idea? It's a good school. She'd get opportunities there she'd never have otherwise."

"That's not the point."

"I know. But Cash is never going to forgive you. Not for stealing my heart. Not for losing Colt to Destiny. Not for baby Marigold, who might very well end up inheriting everything."

A thought flickers through my mind—did Colt do this on purpose? Get Destiny pregnant to secure a claim on the Ashby fortune?

But I brush it away. That's too calculated, and the last thing Colt is, is calculating.

"Cash wants you to fight him for Mercy," I explain, my hand sliding down to his chest. "He knows he'll win. He's paying off judges to rule in his favor."

Legion's jaw clenches, but his eyes soften as my fingers trace the outline of his scar.

"Let Cash think he won," I whisper, my hand

drifting lower, over his ribs. "Let Mercy get all the perks of being part of the Ashby dynasty. Let her go to Rimrock and get a first-class education. Let her keep the puppy, and the pony, and the clothes."

My fingers tease at the waistband of his jeans.

"Let someone else take care of her, you mean?" Legion asks, his voice sharp despite the way his body responds to my touch.

I don't say what we're both thinking—that he's always let other people take care of Mercy. I don't have to. The truth hangs between us, unspoken but also undeniable.

Legion's shoulders slump slightly. "I've never been there for Mercy. Or for Destiny. But I'm back now."

"I know you are." I step closer, pressing myself against him. "But being back doesn't mean you have to fight every battle the hard way."

His hands find my waist, grip tightening. "You're saying I should just give up. Let Cash win."

"I'm saying pick your battles." I tilt my head back to meet his eyes. "You can't win this one, Legion. Not through the courts. Not with your record and your... lifestyle."

"My lifestyle." He says it flat, emotionless.

My heart aches for him. Legion isn't a demon. He's not. He's a good man. He tries hard. And he's loyal as fuck. I place my hands on his face, pull his gaze down to mine. Make him look me in the eyes.

"In the flesh, Legion Kane, you are perfect just the way you are. I wouldn't change a thing."

He rolls his eyes at me. "But…"

"But… on paper, you're Demon, member of one

Badlands MC. Ex-con. Felon. And the courts, Legion, that's all they see. That's all they'll ever see."

"Right. Because I'm trash." His grip loosens. "Trailer trash with prison ink."

"Don't put words in my mouth. I chose you. I got your name tattooed on my wrist. I let you claim me in front of your entire club. I'm just tryin' to figure out how we survive this without losing everything that matters."

Legion's jaw works. He's angry, but not at me. Not really.

"Let her live here. Let Cash spoil her. She's never gonna love him. Like him, maybe. But he's not you, Legion. And you're the one she loves. You're the one she'll fight for. Let her stay. Let her go to school at Rimrock. And then… you'll feel like you belong."

He side-eyes me. "Like I belong… where?"

"Here." I point to the ground. "With me. And Mercy."

He looks off into the distance for a moment, thinking. I give him time. It's a good two minutes before he finds my gaze again. "What about work?"

"Work?" And again, I am reminded that I don't actually know what he does for work. "Well… yeah. You can work. Of course. You could help me."

"Help you do what, Savannah?" For a moment, I think he's angry. But then, he picks up my hand and kisses my knuckles. Eyes locked on mine. "Is making you scream my name while I fuck you blind something I can apply for?"

I chuckle. "It goes without sayin' that's your number

one job here. But seriously, Legion. There's lots of things you could do on the ranch."

His eyes narrow at me. "Like what?"

"Like… ranch handin'. We could do it together. I like ranch handin'. Or… business stuff. That's mostly what I do. Social media, stuff like that." Sensing this is not the answer he was lookin' for, I improvise. "Or… rebuild cars. Bikes. Do you do stuff like that? I feel like your clothes often have the scent of cars on them. Is that your job at the club? Do you work with Ratchet? Speaking of the club, June has called several times over the past two weeks asking about you. I think we're friends now. How do you like that? I've got myself a biker-woman friend."

He smiles. Kisses my knuckles again. Squeezes my hand. "I love you, Savannah. You're all I've ever wanted."

"And you're all I've ever wanted too." My heart swells with warmth and I let out a breath.

This might work.

We gather our stuff up and walk back to the Jeep.

And I can't remember a time when I felt this happy.

CHAPTER 10
LEGION

I grip the Willys Jeep's steering wheel, feelin' every bump and rattle through my palms as we head back to the Ashby mansion. The gearbox whines when I shift, and the engine growls like something half-wild. The wind rushes through the open sides, tearing at Savannah's hair, turning it into a golden flag.

The sun hangs low against the eastern horizon, casting long shadows across the badlands. The landscape stretches out, all jagged edges and cracked earth. Broken land. Forgotten land.

I think about Martinez, this guy from Boston I met inside. Used to bitch constantly about Montana. Called it "God's ashtray" and a "waste of fucking air." Said only people with nothing left to lose would choose to live in a place so ugly.

A lot of the Montana boys wanted to beat his ass for that. Not me. I got what he was saying. This place isn't pretty like forests or oceans. It's honest. Brutal. The badlands don't lie to you about what they are.

I've never wanted to leave. Never dreamed of California beaches or New York lights. I just want my own corner of this hellhole where I can breathe without someone's boot on my neck.

The sky above us swirls with thunderheads, purple and blue, almost black in places. Storm's coming. I can smell it—that metallic tang that hangs in the air before rain hits dry dirt. The wind picks up, carrying dust across the road in thin, dancing spirals.

I keep turning over what Savannah said earlier. About Mercy. About Cash.

The Jeep's engine roars as we climb a hill, drowning out any possibility of conversation. Which is fine by me because I need to think.

Is it Cash I hate? Or just the idea of anyone else raising Mercy? Both, probably.

Cash Ashby with his pressed shirts and his fucking Stetson. The way he looks at me like I'm somethin' he found on the bottom of his boot. The beatings. The threats. The way he left me to die.

But it's more than that. It's Mercy calling someone else for help when she's scared. It's someone else teaching her to ride, to shoot, to stand up for herself. It's someone else being there when she has nightmares.

It's me failing. Again.

We turn onto the long drive leading to the Ashby mansion, and I see them right away. Mercy on a stocky brown pony, trotting around the main arena. Not the dirt round pen where the ranch hands work their horses. The fancy one, with the perfect sand footing and the black rails.

Cash stands at the fence, one boot propped on the

bottom rail. He's calling out instructions, gesturing with one hand. Even from here, I can see Mercy bouncing in the saddle, her back stiff, her hands too high. She looks like she's riding a jackhammer, not a horse.

I wince. Kid's gonna be sore tomorrow.

"She's doing great," Savannah says, breaking into my thoughts. "Especially for a beginner. Look at how she keeps trying."

I grunt, not trusting myself to speak.

"She loves it," Savannah continues. "And that's what matters. Riding hurts at first—every muscle aches, and you fall. A lot. She's already come off twice since she started."

I snap my head toward her. "She fell off?"

Savannah smiles. "I can't even count how many times I've fallen. Most kids give up after the first time. The ones who get back on? Those are the horse girls. They'll give up everything—time, money, sleep—just to be around horses."

I hear what she's not saying. This is good for Mercy. Rimrock Academy would be good for her. A place where she could ride every day, learn from professionals. Not like the trailer. Not like the club.

"The best thing about having a horse-girl sister," Savannah says, "is they don't think about boys."

That pulls a laugh from me. "Bullshit. You were the biggest horse girl I ever met, and you were boy-crazy as hell."

She leans into me, her hands wrapping around my bicep, her body warm against mine. Her lips brush my cheek, soft and quick. "I've only ever been crazy about one boy," she whispers.

This makes me smile. A real one. Something genuine that starts in my chest and works its way up. She's always been able to do that. Pull something real from me when everything else feels like a performance.

I watch her settle back into her seat, hair whipping around her face in the wind, and my mind drifts to all the ways she's changed since we were kids. How she went from the shy girl who blushed when I held her hand to the woman who fucked me in front of an entire club of outlaws without blinking.

Savannah Ashby wasn't always like this. Not as a teenager. Back then, everything was slow and careful. Like we had all the time in the world to figure things out. To be in love. To make love.

Then she went away to college.

First time she came back on break, she met me at the silo like always. But something had shifted. She was desperate, hungry. Wouldn't even let me say hello before she was tearing at my belt, dropping to her knees on that dirty concrete floor.

I remember standing there, shocked stupid, as she took me in her mouth for the first time. Her hands trembling but determined, her eyes locked on mine like she was proving something.

And while I enjoyed it—fucking immensely—I was surprised at her intensity. Couldn't help picturing all the college boys she'd been practicing on. All those rich pricks with their clean hands and pressed shirts. The thought made me want to put my fist through the wall.

But it was like she was reading my mind, because she pulled back, lips swollen, and told me I was her first. That she'd never done this before.

I didn't want to believe her. Pride, maybe. Or just the need to protect myself from how much that would mean.

But she gagged a lot when she took me deeper. Kept having to stop and catch her breath. She wasn't good at it—not then. Not like now, when she knows exactly how to take me apart with her mouth. She knows exactly how far my cock can slide down her throat.

And anyway, her word is good enough for me. Why would I want to call her a liar? Deep down, I've always wanted to be the only man she was ever with. Stupid as that sounds.

The Jeep bounces over a rut in the road, jarring me back to the present. We're approaching the ranch house now, that massive log monstrosity with its perfect symmetry and endless windows. I've never felt more out of place than I do on Ashby land.

I park near the side entrance, cut the engine, and swing out of the driver's seat. My chest still aches, but it's a lot better than it was just a couple days ago. And nothin' near the constant fire it was the day I got here.

I walk around to Savannah's side and take her hand when she offers it. But instead of leading me inside like I expect, she pulls me toward the riding arena where Mercy's lesson is still going on.

My feet drag a little. I don't want a confrontation with Cash. Not with Mercy watching. Not when I'm still weak enough that he might actually win if things get physical.

But Savannah's grip is firm, her smile determined as she tugs me forward. "Come on," she says. "Let's show your sister how proud you are."

So I let her do it. Let her pull me toward the arena, my boots kicking gravel like it's dread. The riding arena rises before us—all perfect black rails and manicured sand. Everything the Ashbys touch, turns expensive. Even dirt.

Mercy spots us and starts waving frantically, her little body bouncing in the saddle of a stocky pony with a wild mane. Her smile stretches ear to ear, the kind of genuine happiness I haven't seen on her face since long before I went inside.

"Eyes forward!" Cash barks from the edge of the ring. "Watch where you're going, not who's watching!"

The pony tosses its head, sensing Mercy's distraction. Her balance shifts. For a second, my heart seizes—she's going to fall. I take a half-step forward, useless at this distance, as the pony sidesteps sharply.

"Heels down, Mercy!" Savannah's voice cuts through the air, clear and commanding. "Look between his ears, not at us!"

Mercy's face snaps forward, her body correcting itself. The pony settles immediately.

Savannah slips between the rails like she was born doing it—which she was—and crosses to a tall woman in riding pants who must be the instructor. Madeline, I think her name is. They fall into easy conversation, laughing and gesturing as they both call out instructions to Mercy.

Which leaves me standing alone with Cash Ashby.

The man who beat me unconscious, left me to die tied to a support beam, and orchestrated my sister's kidnapping through the family court system. Not to mention, sanctioned the kidnapping of his own fuckin' sister.

This is the man Savannah wants me to trust?

What a joke.

Neither of us says a word.

The air between us feels charged, like the moment before lightning strikes. My muscles tense, ready for whatever comes. Cash stands with his thumbs hooked in his belt loops, Stetson pulled low over his eyes.

"I like your sister," he says finally, his voice level. No emotion I can read.

I take him in properly for the first time since that night at the cabin. Cash Ashby stands six-feet-four in his custom boots, shoulders broad from actual ranch work, not just gym time. His face is all hard angles, tanned from days outside. Blue eyes—Savannah's eyes—cold as winter under the shadow of his hat brim.

"She's a quick learner," he continues when I don't respond. "Natural seat. Good hands."

I watch Mercy trot a circle, her face set in concentration. "She's a Kane," I say, like that explains everything.

Cash makes a sound that might be a laugh or just air escaping. "I missed most of Savannah's childhood," he says, surprising me with the shift. "Her riding lessons. Her first shows." He nods toward the arena. "All this. I was away at school, then college, then working the northern properties."

His gaze stays fixed on the riders, but I can feel the weight of something unsaid.

"Eleanor's fault," he adds. "She kept us apart. Kept

all of us apart from Savannah. Too busy turning her into content."

The bitterness in his voice catches me off guard. I've spent years hating the Ashbys as a unit—one solid wall of privilege and disdain. Never considered they might have their own fractures, their own wounds.

"I never understood my mother," Cash says, eyes still on the arena. Then he turns, fixing me with a stare that feels hot. "But you did, didn't you?"

The question hangs between us, dangerous as a lit fuse.

I'm not afraid of Cash Ashby. Even injured, I figure I could take him if it came to it. But there's something in his tone that isn't confrontation. It's almost... resignation.

Maybe I do owe him some kind of explanation. Not for his sake, but for what lies between us. For Savannah. For Mercy, who's laughing now as she tries her best to post the pony's trot.

"Yeah," I say, lookin' down at my boots. "I did understand your mother. There was a time there... when I think... I was her best friend."

Cash's jaw tightens, then releases. "Did you fuck my mother?"

The question is so blunt, so unexpected, that a laugh escapes me before I can stop it. Not amusement—more like disbelief that we're having this conversation while watching a nine-year-old's riding lesson.

"Even if I did," I tell him, meeting his gaze directly, "I'd answer that question with a lie."

Something flickers across his face—anger, confusion,

maybe even respect. Hard to tell because I don't really know him.

I've said all I'm going to say on the subject.

Eleanor Ashby's ghost doesn't get to haunt this moment too.

I turn away from Cash, slip between the arena rails, and cross the perfect sand to where Savannah stands with Madeline. My boots leave heavy prints in the carefully groomed surface.

Savannah's smile when she sees me approach feels like the only real thing in this artificial world they've built.

I stand beside her, close enough that our arms touch, and watch my little sister ride circles around all the things we're not saying.

CHAPTER 11
SAVANNAH

I don't know what Cash said to Legion, but something shifted between them. Legion's face when he joins me in the center of the arena is carefully blank—that prison mask he wears when he's processing something he doesn't want me to see.

"Legion, this is Madeline," I say, gesturing to my riding instructor. "She's been teaching Mercy this past week."

Madeline extends her hand. "Pleasure to meet you. Your sister has remarkable natural ability."

Legion nods and shakes her hand. "Thanks for teaching her." His voice is polite but distant, eyes already tracking Mercy as she tries her best to post the trot.

And that's it.

Those are the last words he says. I almost expect him to leave, but he doesn't. He holds my hand. Standing easily next to me as he watches Mercy. Mercy calls things out to him, but he doesn't answer. Like he's deep in thought.

When the lesson is over, Mercy hops off, beaming with pride when Madeline praises her straight back and light hands. "Did you see me?" she keeps asking Legion. "Did you see how much better I'm getting'?" She's breathless, cheeks flushed with excitement.

Legion ruffles her hair. "Looked pretty good to me, Merce."

"Can I show you my room? I have my own bathroom and everything!"

Legion glances at me, then back to Mercy. "Lead the way."

I thank Madeline when she offers to put the pony away, then follow legion and Mercy inside, and up the grand staircase. But once up there, I hand back a little as Mercy pulls Legion through the door of what used to be a guest suite.

She's transformed it completely in just ten days—horse posters cover the walls, stuffed animals crowd the bed, riding boots lined up beneath the window seat.

I watch Legion's face, expecting anger or at least sadness. This is everything he couldn't give her. Everything the Ashbys have that the Kanes don't. But instead, he smiles as Mercy shows him all the stuff we got out of he attic. Her collection of horse figurines that used to be mine, her books that used to be mine, the fancy riding gear I grew out of almost two decades ago.

I hadn't really realized that Eleanor kept everything from my childhood up in the rambling three-thousand square-foot attic.

And I do mean everything.

Like this stuff would be important one day. Collectable.

I'd rather it be used and thrown out than turn into a listing on Ebay.

"And look!" Mercy pulls open her closet door. "I have so many clothes now! And shoes that actually fit!" All those are new. The clothes from my childhood, while still in this house, are not fit to wear two decades later.

"It's all real nice, Mercy," Legion says, and I can tell he means it. He's not bitter or jealous. He's just glad she's happy.

I hadn't realized how much I was bracing for a fight until it doesn't come. Cash has been spoiling Mercy relentlessly—partly to win her over, partly to spite Legion. I expected some push back from that.

But he is rather calm about the whole thing. Calm enough that I figure I can slip away. "I'm going to freshen up for dinner," I say, needing a moment to recalibrate. "Legion, we eat at seven."

He nods, already being dragged toward Mercy's bathroom to see her collection of fancy soaps shaped like animals.

In my room, I strip and step into the shower, letting hot water wash away the canyon dust and dried sweat from our afternoon together. I close my eyes, remembering the way Legion's hands felt on my skin. How perfectly we fit together. How his eyes stayed locked on mine the entire time we were fucking, like he was memorizing every reaction, every sound I made.

But underneath that perfect moment was the reality

we're still avoiding. He wants to go back to his trailer. Back to the club that abandoned him when he needed them most. And I want...

I don't know what I want anymore. Not the life my mother planned for me, certainly. Not Marcus White and his political aspirations. Not the endless performance of being Savannah Ashby, Instagram royalty.

Just Legion. And Mercy. And some kind of peace.

After freshening up, I go down to the kitchen to grab Legion's dinner tray. It's something I've taken to doing since he's been here. Even though I've never been much of a lunch person, three times a day the three of us, Mercy, Legion, and I, gather together for food.

It's been nice. Almost like a real family.

Of course, this is not an unusual thing for me. The Ashbys have been gathering for meals for hundreds of years and all the chairs were always full.

Most years, anyway. Before Eleanor died.

But having dinner as an Ashby and having dinner as a Kane are two completely different things.

I learned early in Mercy's stay that children do not fuck around in the this-is-what-I-will-and-will-not-eat department. The kitchen staff brought Mercy a grilled chicken salad for lunch the first time I was home from the hospital at lunchtime after Legion woke up. She didn't throw a fit, per se. But it was Mercy's version of one. She crossed her arms and shook her head. All the while that upper lip was sneering at that salad.

Cash was there. He was a tiny bit exasperated with

her. "Mercy," he barked, "this is what's being served for lunch. This is the meal. You will eat it."

Of course, she defied him. Shaking her head and stiffening that upper lip even more.

Cash, to his credit, seemed to be trying hard to be nice to her. Why that is, I have no idea. Probably because I was there and he wanted to make me think he was in control of the situation.

But he wasn't. She didn't eat that salad. Or the one that came with dinner, which was burgers that night. She ate those just fine.

So the next day, I asked the kitchen staff to make her child-friendly lunches. Cash didn't argue. I secretly think he's relieved that I'm here, kinda takin' over.

Cash's personality change has been both revealing and surprising. Because he generally seems to like Mercy. I'm not sure what happened in those first days she was here alone with him, while Legion was dyin' and I was frantically trying to keep him alive.

ut something did happen between them. Because Mercy generally seems to like Cash as well. She doesn't have conversations with him the way she does with me, but she seems to respect my oldest brother in a way I can't quite understand.

Perhaps it was the puppy. Or all the clothes in her new closet. Or the new bedroom decorated for a pre-teen girl that did not exist in our house until Mercy came to live in it.

Regardless, she likes him and I think he likes her back. Which is why I took his side about Rimrock Academy.

"You loved it there," he told me, after I learned of his

plan. "You know you loved it there. You came home every Friday afternoon with regret, Savannah."

"Well," I laughed. "Eleanor's digital prison never felt like a home." He was right though. I did hate coming home from the academy on the weekends. I would've rather stayed on campus. But Eleanor didn't permit it. The car appeared for me every Friday at two-thirty and back I came.

Of course, I did like seeing Legion on the weekends. But he didn't appear in my life until I was twelve and I didn't go proper boy-crazy over him for three more years after that. He wasn't a part of my formative years, Rimrock was.

So yes, I do think the academy is a good fit for Mercy. She's a bit feral and she won't fit in—at first. But she's adjusted remarkably well to the posh life. She's not a girl who gets put off by bribes. Perhaps she doesn't know that Cash is bribing her with puppies and ponies, but I think she does.

And I think she likes it.

She doesn't talk back to him. She doesn't talk back to anyone. I think Mercy Kane understands that she fell into a Cinderella story and she's not about to let this opportunity slip away without a fight.

I don't blame her.

No offense to Legion, but Mercy's childhood has been a complete shit-show. The movie-of-the-week on Lifetime can't hold a candle to this child's drama.

When I get to the kitchen, there is no dinner tray set up for Legion. "Excuse me, Ms. Charlot? Do you know when Legion's dinner tray will be ready?"

"Oh, he's eating in the dining room tonight, Miss Savannah."

"Is he?" I exclaim.

"Yes," Ms. Charlot says, chuckling a bit at my reaction. "I'm just about to serve, if you'd like to take your seat at the table."

I smile. He's eating at the dinner table. With Cash. Not Wyatt, he's practically disappeared since Legion came, but I've never been close with Wyatt.

Cash is enough though. Because it's just been over a month since that whole kidnapping thing. And I was pretty sure Legion was going to enact some kind of revenge against Cash about it, but there has been no confrontation.

Which should not surprise me, actually. Legion, I've noticed, is not really a confrontational man. He's quiet. Always watching, always listening, but he's not reactive. Posturing isn't something he does.

He's always been like that though. Typically, a man of few words. But also a man of action. When he makes his mind up about something, it's done and there's no goin' back.

"OK," I tell Ms. Charlot. "I'll go take my seat. Thank you so much."

I leave the kitchen smiling. Feeling pretty OK with this moment. Marcus hasn't bothered me, Legion is going to live, Mercy is happy, and even Cash seems satisfied for the moment.

This might be the most peaceful I've felt in years.

I enter the dining room and stop just inside the doorway, taking in the scene. Cash sits at the head of the table, where he's sat since Eleanor died. Mercy's sitting on his right, her legs swinging back and forth beneath the chair, not quite reaching the floor. And Legion—my tattooed, scarred, just-barely-survived-sepsis Legion—is sitting across from her, on Cash's left.

All three of them look up when I enter. But it's Legion who pushes his chair back and stands. He crosses to me in three long strides and kisses me on the cheek, his lips warm against my skin.

"Hey," he says quietly, just for me.

Then he's pulling my chair out—the one next to his, across from Mercy—and waiting for me to sit.

I blink, momentarily frozen. Legion's never pulled out a chair for me. Not once in all the years I've known him. I'm not even sure he's ever seen anyone pull out a chair for anyone else. It's not exactly standard procedure at the Badlands clubhouse.

"Thank you," I murmur, sitting down as he pushes the chair in behind me.

I'm still processing this unexpected gesture when Ms. Charlot appears with steaming plates of lasagna, setting them down in front of each of us before returning with a basket of bread and a large bowl of salad.

The food looks incredible—layers of pasta, meat, and cheese with perfectly browned edges. Mercy doesn't waste any time, immediately digging in with the enthusiasm of someone who's spent most of her life never knowing when the next meal might come.

The table falls silent except for the sound of forks against plates. The quiet stretches just a beat too long, becoming that specific kind of awkward that happens when four people who probably shouldn't be eating together find themselves doing exactly that.

I open my mouth to ask about the weather or something equally banal when Cash beats me to it.

"Mercy," he says, cutting his lasagna into perfect squares, "did you look through that school catalog I gave you yet?"

My fingers tighten around my fork. I glance at Legion, expecting to see his jaw clench or his shoulders tense. But he's just... eating. Focused on his food like Cash hasn't just deliberately brought up the one topic guaranteed to cause friction.

Mercy, however, lights up instantly. "Yes! I read the whole thing. Twice." She sits up straighter, fork momentarily forgotten. "They have a science lab with real microscopes, and an equestrian program with thirty horses, and a climbing wall in the gym and—"

She continues rattling off facts about Rimrock while I watch Legion from the corner of my eye. He continues eating methodically, seemingly unbothered by the conversation happening around him. This is not the reaction I expected. Not even close.

Cash takes a sip of his water, his eyes fixed on Legion over the rim of his glass. "What do you think about Rimrock Academy, Legion?" he asks, setting the glass down with deliberate care. "For Mercy's education."

I hold my breath. Here it comes. The explosion. The argument. The end of this strange, fragile peace.

But Legion just looks up from his plate, a small smile playing at the corners of his mouth. He turns to Mercy—not Cash—and says, "I think it's a great idea, sis."

The smile that breaks across Mercy's face is like nothing I've ever seen from her. Pure, unfiltered joy.

"Really?" she practically shouts, bouncing in her seat. "You mean it?"

"I do," Legion says, nodding once.

"Did you know," Mercy continues, words tumbling out faster than she can form them, "they have uniforms? Real ones with plaid skirts and everything! And the dorms—you get to stay the night! All week long! You only have to come home on weekends!"

She says this last part like it's the most exciting thing imaginable, not seeming to realize what it means—that she'd be away from Legion five days a week. Or maybe she does realize it, and that's part of the appeal. A clean break from her old life, even if just Monday through Friday.

I watch Legion's face carefully, searching for any sign that this hurts him. But if it does, he doesn't show it.

Maybe this is it, then?

Maybe this is how we keep the peace?

Mercy goes away to a good school where she wants to be.

Cash gets to pretend he's altruistic.

And Legion and I can… well… start our lives. We don't have to live here. I'll happily live at his trailer. I don't mind at all. I mean, I don't really have a job, exactly. I maintain the social media sites just because…

well, they're worth a lot as far as reach goes. And people genuinely seem to like what I do—which is nothin' really. Odd. But I guess watching someone else live their life makes it easier to ignore your own.

I can do that from anywhere.

All I need is a phone.

CHAPTER 12
LEGION

I stand in the hallway outside Mercy's room, watching her sleep through the cracked door. The mansion's quiet presses against my ears—no shouting neighbors, no bikes firing up at 3 AM, no thin walls carrying every sound. Just silence thick enough to drown in.

Mercy's riding boots sit by her dresser, caked with arena sand but lined up neatly. Never seen her arrange anything that precisely before. Her helmet hangs on some fancy custom hook. Her backpack leans against the desk, zipped tight and ready for school in a few weeks.

Her hair spreads across the pillow, finally brushed proper. No more tangles for me to try to comb out while she squirmed and cursed like a miniature sailor. No wishing our mother was still alive to handle these things.

She's clutching that Rimrock catalog to her chest. Not the BB gun. A school catalog.

And she's just sleeping. Like a kid should.

Three days from now, she'll be fitted for uniforms with the Ashby black card. In three weeks, she'll walk through those academy gates with her head high, backpack filled with a tablet and a phone.

The truth hits me hard. She's safer here than she's ever been with me.

I close the door with a soft click, step back, and exhale.

I hesitate at Savannah's door, hand frozen on the knob. She went to bed about an hour ago while I went outside for some air—a cigarette, really. At least that's what Savannah thought. I did smoke, but all I really wanted was some time to think.

Now, thinkin's over.

The door opens without a sound. Closes the same way. Rich people hinges. No creaking to announce you're coming or going.

Savannah lies there watching me, moonlight spilling across her like water. Her hair fans out on the pillow, blue eyes tracking me in the darkness. She lifts her hand, palm up. Waiting.

I cross to her, feeling like I'm walking through someone else's life. The floor doesn't creak. The air smells like lavender, not mold.

I take her hand, lowering myself to the edge of her bed. The mattress barely dips under my weight. My bare chest feels exposed in the moonlight—all those tattoos telling stories I've never explained to her. The archangel over my heart. The demons writhing beneath its sword. The bone court. The scorch line. The tally marks nobody understands.

Savannah's fingers find the archangel, tracing where

the flaming sword pierces straight through the horned beast's chest. Her touch is cool against the scar tissue where my brand is finally healing.

I take her hand, bringing it to my lips. Press a kiss into her palm. Her pulse jumps against my mouth.

"Savannah," I whisper, not sure what else to say.

She rises up on her knees, the silk nightgown sliding against her skin. I reach for the hem, lifting it slowly. She raises her arms, letting me pull it over her head. The moonlight paints her naked body silver and shadow.

I run my fingertips down her throat, across her collarbone, down to where her heartbeat hammers beneath her skin. She shivers under my touch. My hands feel too rough for her, but she never flinches from them. Never has.

"Come here," she whispers, and I do.

I lay her back against the pillows, moving over her like a shadow. My lips find her neck, her shoulder, the hollow of her throat. She tastes like honey and salt. Like every good thing I never deserved.

I trail my mouth down her body, taking my time. My tongue circles one nipple, then the other, feeling them harden against me. Her fingers tangle in my hair, not pulling, just holding on. Like I'm something worth keeping.

Lower I go, mapping the terrain of her ribs, the soft dip of her belly, the curve of her hip. I slide my hands beneath her, lifting her up to my mouth. Her thighs part for me, and I settle between them, breathing her in.

The first touch of my tongue makes her gasp. I go slow, tasting her like I'm memorizing the flavor. And I am. Every sound she makes, every tremor that runs through her body, I'm storing it all away. For when this ends. For when she realizes what I've always known—that I'm just a placeholder until something better comes along.

But right now, she's mine. All mine.

Her hips rise to meet my mouth. I hold her steady, my hands spanning her waist as I lick into her, finding the rhythm that makes her breath catch. She's so wet against my tongue, so ready. Her hands fist in the sheets, then in my hair, then back to the sheets.

"Legion," she breathes, and my name in her mouth sounds like something holy.

I feel her getting close, her thighs tensing around my head, her breathing shallow and quick. I pull back, not ready for this to end. Not ready to let her go.

She makes a sound of protest that turns into a sigh as I move up her body, kissing my way back to her mouth. She tastes herself on my lips, and it makes her moan.

I yank my sweats down, position myself between her legs, the head of my cock sliding against her slickness. Her eyes lock with mine as I push inside, slow and steady, until I'm buried. "Fuck," I whisper against her temple, overwhelmed by the feel of her around me. Tight, and hot, and perfect.

I start to move, each thrust measured and deep. Not rushing. Not chasing. Just feeling every inch of her wrapped around every inch of me.

Her hands slide down my back, tracing the angels and demons inked into my skin. Touching the scars, the stories, the marks of a life lived hard, and fast, and without grace.

But there's grace here now. In the way she touches me. In the way she sees me.

I watch her face as I move inside her. The way her lips part. The flutter of her eyelashes. The flush that spreads across her cheeks and down her throat.

"Savannah," I whisper, her name the only prayer I know.

She arches beneath me, taking me deeper, her legs wrapping around my waist. I slide my hand between us, finding that spot that makes her cry out. My thumb circles it in time with my thrusts, and I feel her start to tighten around me.

"Look at me," I tell her, and she does, her eyes finding mine in the darkness. "Stay with me."

She nods, holding my gaze as her body begins to pulse around my cock. I watch every flicker of pleasure cross her face, every gasp and sigh and silent scream. It's the most beautiful thing I've ever seen.

I follow her over the edge, spilling into her with a groan that comes from somewhere deep inside me. Somewhere I thought was empty until she filled it.

Savannah fits against me like she was carved from my rib. She curls into my side, her head finding that hollow beneath my shoulder where it's always belonged. Her breathing slows, but her fingers don't. They keep moving, tracing the tally marks etched near my collarbone like she's trying to count them. Like she's trying to understand what each one means.

She won't. Nobody does. Not even Diesel, who's seen me add to them.

One mark for each time I should've died but didn't. One mark for each debt I'll never repay. One mark for each sin I've committed that can't be washed away.

I've stopped counting. Just keep adding.

Her fingers finally still against my skin. Her breathing deepens, evens out. Sleep claims her while I'm still wide awake, my mind racing like an engine redlining.

She clings to me even in sleep. Her arm draped across my chest, leg hooked over mine, like she's afraid I'll disappear if she lets go.

And she should be.

Fear's the only rational response to a man like me.

I stare at the ceiling, watching shadows from the trees outside dance across it. This room is bigger than my entire trailer. The sheets smell like fabric softener, not cigarettes and motor oil. Everything here is clean, soft, expensive.

Everything except me.

Her grip tightens in her sleep, fingers digging into my ribs. I recognize fear when I feel it. Been the cause of it often enough. She's afraid—of what I mean, what I bring, the darkness that follows me like a shadow. The danger I carry isn't something you can lock outside with fancy security systems and gates.

It's in my blood. In my name.

The tattoos across my back press into the mattress beneath me. The angels, the demons, the eternal war—all of them watching, judging. Reminding me of every decision I've made that led me here. Every failure. Every inevitable betrayal waiting to happen.

The archangel on my chest seems to burn, like it

knows I don't belong here. Like it knows I'm just pretending. Playing house in a mansion while my brothers at the club turn their backs on me. While Cash watches from the shadows, waiting for me to fuck up so he can take Mercy for good.

While Savannah dreams of a life I can never give her.

I don't sleep. Don't even try. Just lie there counting her breaths instead, memorizing the rhythm. One-two-three-pause. One-two-three-pause. Storing it away for the long nights ahead when I'll be alone again, staring at a different ceiling, remembering how it felt to hold something clean, and whole, and good in these bloodstained hands.

Her hair spills across my chest like honey. I touch it carefully, afraid to wake her. It's so soft, it barely feels real. Nothing about this feels real.

Not the linen sheets. Not the moonlight streaming through windows without bars. Not the woman sleeping in my arms like I'm something worth holding onto.

Especially not the choice I've already made.

Mercy's getting her shot. The education, the horses, the chance to be something more than a Kane. The chance to break the curse that's followed our bloodline for generations.

And Savannah... Savannah gets her freedom. From Marcus. From her brothers. From her mother's ghost and all those photographs.

From me.

She mumbles something in her sleep, burrowing closer. I wrap my arm around her, holding her tight against me. Memorizing the weight of her. The smell of her hair. The way her breath feels against my skin.

Outside, an owl calls into the darkness. Another answers. They speak a language I don't understand, but it sounds like a warning.

I close my eyes, not to sleep but to focus. To remember this moment exactly as it is. To burn it into my memory alongside all the other things I've lost.

All the other things I've walked away from.

All the other things I've destroyed.

The tally marks on my collarbone seem to itch.

Like they're waiting for me to add another.

One more debt I'll never repay.

One more sin that can't be washed away.

One more time I should die, but won't.

I ease myself from beneath Savannah's sleeping form, careful not to wake her. Her body shifts, seeking my warmth, then settles back into the expensive sheets with a sigh. The floorboards don't creak here—nothing in the Ashby mansion announces itself. Nothing betrays.

The moon hangs low over the eastern pasture, spilling silver across acres of land that will never know my footprints. I stand at the window, bare-chested, watching my reflection watch me back. The brand over my heart stands out, the angry red starting to turn white now.

I trace the invisible 'B' with my fingertips. The skin puckers under my touch, sensitive and wrong. I remember the sizzle of my flesh, the smell of burning skin, Brick's eyes shining with pride when I didn't scream. When I took it like a man.

Like a brother.

Beyond the glass, Ashby land stretches for miles in perfectly maintained fences and manicured fields. The stables stand silent in the distance, housing horses worth more than I can even comprehend. Nothing here knows hunger or need. Nothing here understands survival.

I place my palm flat against the cool window, marking the barrier between my world and hers. The glass feels cold and unyielding. Like the truth.

After dinner, Mercy showed me the Rimrock catalog. Her small fingers traced over pictures of girls in plaid skirts clustered around a science display. Her eyes had widened with excitement as she described the paleontology club and their collection of real dinosaur bones.

"They have an actual triceratops skull, Legion. And they let the kids touch it!"

She'd never had possibilities in the trailer. Just survival—instant noodles, second-hand clothes, and learning to shoot before even being legally allowed to hunt. Her whole life, watching doors close before she even knew they existed.

I glance back at Savannah. She could have anyone—a man with clean hands and a clean record. Someone who wouldn't drag death and danger behind him like a shadow. Someone who belongs in this house, with its crystal glasses and imported rugs.

The brand stretches when I move. Tight and taut, reminding me of the promise I made. The brotherhood that took me in when no one else would. The life that fits a man with my history, my violence, my particular set of skills.

I turn back to the window, seeing my reflection merge with the distant mountains pressing my forehead against the glass, feeling the cold seep into my skin. I don't belong here among linen sheets and security systems. I belong in the dirt with my brothers, doing the ugly work that keeps the wheels turning. This brief taste of another life was never meant to last.

Just a fever dream.

Just one more thing to lose.

Back downstairs in my room, I dress in darkness, jeans, t-shirt, boots.

Moonlight spills through tall windows, illuminating the Ashby dynasty in silver frames. Eleanor's eyes follow me from every photograph, knowing and possessive. I don't look at them directly. Some ghosts are better left undisturbed.

The kitchen is all granite and stainless steel, everything cold and perfect. The landline hangs on the wall—old school, like something from another time. My fingers dial without hesitation, the number etched into my bones since I was seventeen, desperate to belong somewhere.

Three rings before Diesel answers, his voice rough with sleep or whiskey or both. "Yeah?"

"It's me," I keep my voice low, though no one in this house would hear a gunshot through these thick walls. "I need a ride."

The silence stretches between us, filled with what I'm not saying.

"From the Ashby place?" He finally asks, judgment thick in his tone.

"Yeah. Bring the Charger, not your bike."

Another pause. I can almost hear him weighing his response.

"Trouble?"

I close my eyes, seeing Savannah's face when she wakes to find me gone. Seeing Mercy's when she realizes I've left again.

"No. Just time."

Diesel breathes into the phone, understanding what I mean. The club doesn't require explanations. Doesn't demand justifications for the damage you carry. My demons fit there, contained within rules, and hierarchy, and purpose.

"Leavin' now. Be there in forty," he says, and the line goes dead.

I replace the receiver and stand in the perfect kitchen where I don't belong. Where I've never belonged.

Then I leave without saying goodbye.

The gravel crunches beneath my boots as I walk the quarter-mile drive. I pull a crumpled pack of Marlboros from my pocket, bummed earlier from one of the ranch hands. Light one, the flame briefly illuminating my face in the darkness. The first drag burns all the way down, sharp and familiar.

Halfway to the gate, I stop and turn. The mansion sits dark and silent on its perfect hill, framed by mountains that have watched over this valley for centuries. All that money, all that history, all that fucking privilege—and it couldn't save any of them.

Not Eleanor from her obsessions.

Not Savannah from her mother's plans.

Not even Cash from whatever eats him inside out.

Tomorrow morning, Savannah will wake alone. She'll search the house, calling my name. Then she'll understand.

I exhale a cloud of smoke that disappears into the night air. She'll hate me for this. Mercy too, eventually. The thought settles in my chest like a stone, heavy but necessary. Better they hate me than watch me drag them down. Better they build something without me than burn trying to save me.

I reach the gate and punch in the code. The mechanism clicks, and I push it open manually instead of waiting for the automatic swing.

Stepping beyond the boundary, I leave Ashby land behind. The moment my boot touches public dirt, I feel lighter. Like I've shed something I was never meant to wear.

Then... it's nothing but waiting. Thirty long minutes before I hear the rumble of Diesel's 1970 Dodge Charger in the distance. It grows louder as it climbs the county road toward the ranch. The sound is a promise—of brotherhood, of purpose, of the only family that ever wanted the real me, not some version they could fix, or change, or use.

The headlights appear around the bend, cutting through the darkness with twin beams. I drop my cigarette, crushing it under my heel as the car pulls to a stop beside me. Diesel leans across to push open the passenger door.

My Badlands cut lies folded on the seat, the skull

wrapped in barbed wire visible even in the dim light. I pick it up, feeling the weight of it in my hands. The leather is cool against my fingers as I shrug it on, settling it across my shoulders like armor. The brand on my chest seems to pulse beneath my t-shirt, a reminder of blood oaths and promises made.

I slide into the passenger seat, pulling the door closed behind me. I don't look back at the mansion as Diesel pulls away. Don't need to. I've memorized every inch of what I'm leaving behind—Savannah's skin in moonlight, Mercy's smile when she thought we might be a family, the taste of something I was never meant to keep.

"You good?" Diesel asks, eyes on the road ahead.

I nod once, settling deeper into the seat.

Maybe a better man would stay, but I've never been the better man.

"Yeah," I tell him. "I'm good."

SKULLS & lace

Book of Legion — Badlands MC #5

New York Times Bestselling Author

JA HUSS

They've been stealing moments since they were teenagers, burning for each other in a world that keeps demanding they choose sides. Now it's time.

Necessary reckoning.
Spectacular collision.
Brutal reality.

Time to burn it down, boys.

SKULLS AND LACE

Every prayer gets answered.

Not all of them are from God.

Inside the pages you can expect:

🏍️👖🔥 Outlaw Biker Romance
💎🖤🔧 Rich Girl / Poor Boy
👖🔒🖤 Property Of
🖤🫦⚔️ Morally Gray/Anti-Hero MMC
🔥👁️👖 Obsessed/Possessive MMC
🚫🖤🫦 Forbidden Love
💄💋🖤 Only Her
🖤⚔️🔥 Only Him
💚🏚️🌫️ Childhood Sweethearts
⚔️🔪💀 Touch Her and Die
🔥🌶️👶 Primal Spice
🌀🎬🖤 Secret Relationship

ABOUT THE AUTHOR

JA Huss is a scientist, New York Times and USA Today bestselling author. Her self-published romantasy Sparktopia was named an Audible Editors' Best of the Year selection in 2024, and several of her audiobooks have been nominated for the Audie and SOVA Awards. A 2019 RITA finalist, Huss has also had five books optioned for film and television.

www.ingramcontent.com/pod-product-compliance
Lightning Source LLC
LaVergne TN
LVHW090041080526
838202LV00046B/3912